THE
FORT

THE
FORT

ARIC DAVIS

 THOMAS & MERCER

Text copyright © 2013 Aric Davis
All rights reserved.
Printed in the United States of America.
No part of this book may be reproduced, or stored in a retrieval system, or transmitted in any form or by any means, electronic, mechanical, photo-copying, recording, or otherwise, without express written permission of the publisher.

Design & Illustration: © mecob.org
Cover Photographs:
© Stephen Alvarez/Getty
© Doug Garrabrants/Getty
© Visuals Unlimited, Inc.
/Victor Habbick/Getty
© Sung-Il Kim/Corbis

Published by Thomas & Mercer
PO Box 400818
Las Vegas, NV 89140

ISBN-13: 9781611099393
ISBN-10: 1611099390
Library of Congress Control Number: 2012920543

For Scout

1

The fort was made out of scrap wood that had been harvested from Stan Benchley's old deck by his son, Tim, after the deck had been torn down to be replaced by a patio. Tammy Benchley, Tim's mother and Stan's wife, had decided in what Stan decided mid-project was a fit of madness that her husband could install a patio without professional help. Stan, a teacher by trade and a man who very much valued his summer vacations, found the task to be much harder than his wife had told him it would be. The weather was hot as well, and it quickly became clear to Stan that he would be suffering in the heat of the sun for nearly the entire summer, digging out the earth, replacing it with pea gravel, and slowly leveling the stone patio pavers. By contrast, Tim and his friends Scott and Luke had their project finished much faster.

The fort was roughly twenty feet off the floor of what the boys thought of as the forest, and what most adults in the area thought of as the "eyesore." The base of the fort was made by attaching scrapped four-by-fours to three trimmed pine trees growing within a few feet of each other. The boys were able to place these boards by building ladders into the trees using pieces of cut-up two-by-fours, also scrapped, of course. Using the four-by-fours as their attachment point, the boys slowly made the floor of the fort out of more scrap two-by-fours, measuring, cutting, and then attaching each floorboard to the tops of the four-by-fours.

The first of the three trees was the thickest, and rather than build the fort over the base of a difficult-to-create A-shape, the boys used this larger tree to span as near as possible to the width of the other two. This early step in engineering, suggested by Tim's dad, made the shape of the fort's floor closer to a trapezoid than a square, and helped utilize both the strengths and the positions of the three trees to maximum advantage.

The walls of the fort had been kludged together from a mixture of four-by-fours and a forgotten stack of treated plywood that had been left to rot after a project from another summer, a period Stan Benchley still referred to as the Year of the Shed. The plywood had windows sawed into it at heights appropriate for the boys to look through, and allowed incredible sight lines into the rarely trespassed patch of trees.

When it was finished on June 29, 1987, the fort's floor was eight feet by ten feet, give or take an inch or two. Three separate ladders led up to it, one up each tree, and walls a foot taller than the tallest boy—Scott, five feet, five inches—stood to protect them. Windows with crude shutters had been cut into the walls, and a roof was over their heads to protect them from the elements. The roof and walls were afterthoughts, but it was hard to tell, due to the unlikely but really quite skilled construction work done by the three boys.

At the point of the fort's completion, summer break was only a month old. The Detroit Tigers were finally gaining ground in the standings after another shaky start, the Red Wings were awful as usual, but Steve Yzerman was starting to become a presence on the ice. The Pistons had done better, only to be eliminated in the playoffs by the Boston Celtics, and the Lions' season wasn't being mentioned by anyone but the most die-hard fans. Not that the boys cared about much of that, of course. Summer felt like a living, breathing thing, especially only a third of the way through. It was something to be respected and enjoyed, before its evil sisters, fall and school, came back to haunt them.

On this Monday afternoon, Scott knelt in the fort, controlling his cheek weld on the rifle the way Luke had assured him snipers in Vietnam did. During the last weeks of school, Luke had read a book about Carlos Hathcock, legendary sniper of the Vietnam conflict, and Vietnam had been the game ever since, especially since the fort was completed. Next to Tim, Luke held a Daisy air rifle that had been pumped to maximum capacity, not quite powerful enough to break skin, but enough to hurt if one were shot with it. On the other side of Tim was Scott, currently aiming out the window. The rifle's stock was stuffed into his shoulder, and his nontrigger hand was across his chest and supporting the stock from underneath, the way Scott had seen his stepdad do with his deer rifle.

"You got him lined up?" Tim asked. "He isn't moving. Take the shot!"

"Negative," said Scott. "Still scanning the area for other VC." Scott was scanning for North Vietnamese soldiers in black pajamas, but all he was really doing was moving the barrel of the rifle in every direction that kept it from pointing at the target the boys had borrowed from Scott's stepfather's range bag.

"You see any?" Luke asked in a serious voice, and Tim responded in kind.

"Negative on that, Command. Aside from our target, the area appears clear of VC," Scott said in a slow whisper. "I'm going to take the shot."

"Steady on that rifle, Staff Sergeant," said Tim. "The President wants that man dead." Scott gave Tim a look, and Tim shrugged back at him. Finally, Scott laid the front blade of the sight on top of the center of the bull's-eye, aligning it between the blades of the rear sight. He was breathing even more slowly now, just as his dad and Hathcock, the sniper from the book, had agreed was important when shooting. He slowly eased back the trigger, making sure not to jerk it, and the rifle fired.

Scott and Luke dove to the floor of the fort while Tim tried to get the binoculars to focus on the target. Finally, Tim joined them on the floor. "These binoculars still suck. We're going to have to go down there to see if you got a kill."

All three boys shouldered air rifles before descending down the same ladder, one after the other. After all, there could still be VC in the area, regardless of reports. They walked silently to the target, and when they got there, Scott spit in disgust.

"Another miss?" Luke said. "Are we really going to do this all day? We should all get to shoot a couple times and then go look."

"Won't work," said Scott. "We won't know who shot what. I risked getting in a lot of trouble by taking that target, and we're not going to waste it like a bunch of stupid babies." He looked at his friends, first Tim, and then Luke, to make sure they were taking him seriously. "Besides, half the fun is in pretending that we're really snipers. It wouldn't be as cool if we shot it a few hundred times. That would be like, World War Two machine gunners, or something. We're playing sniper."

"You're right, dude," said Luke. "Sorry. But last time I checked, only queers were last ones back to the fort." He said it as he took off at a gallop, his air rifle bouncing on his back. His friends bounded after him, all of them laughing and the forest vacating life around them as they crashed through the brush, quite unlike the men they had been pretending to be.

2

Tim emerged from the woods into his backyard, a ten-minute walk from the branching of trails that led to the fort and the boys' three homes. His dad was sitting on a folding chair, sitting in front of the still-very-much-in-progress patio, and nursing a beer that was sweating condensation faster than it was being drunk. There was an empty folding seat next to his father, and Tim plopped into it, the late-afternoon sun over the peak of the house instantly beginning to roast his face. Tim moved the chair forward a foot and slouched down. *Problem solved.*

"Your mother means to kill me," said Stan. "Or at least wants me to suffer. I'm not sure yet which. It may be both. Has she told you who she plans to marry when the insurance money runs out?"

"Not yet, Dad. Is it that hard? 'Cause it looks super easy."

"Oh, fruit of my loins, you are beyond lucky that I recall and respect the sanctity of a boy's summer vacation. By all rights, you should have a transfer shovel in your massively blistered hands right now, and you should be moving that enormous pile of rocks in the driveway into this hole. We may avoid church, son, but you should thank God just in case. Trust me. You are very lucky."

"It's not like I'm the only kid," said Tim. "Becca's not helping either."

"Becca and Mom are currently discussing terms of war." Becca was fifteen, and things had been moving toward a serious conflict. Tim wasn't sure exactly why she and his mom hadn't been getting along, only that he didn't expect them to start getting along anytime soon, and he figured boys were at least part of the problem. "And because of that, us menfolk are much better off out here. You can either move rocks or compliment my ability to drink a beer. Choose wisely."

"Looking good, Dad."

"Damn straight."

Tim leaned back in the chair, enjoying the warmth, but even more so, the freedom. As much as his dad griped about the patio, Tim had a feeling his old man was enjoying the freedom from work as well, even if he had ended up with a different sort of work.

"So what were you and your buddies up to today?"

"Shooting at a target with our air rifles."

"Vietnam?"

"No."

"Yes," Stan said, then took a drink of beer. "Which is fine with me, by the way. Just don't let Mom catch wind of it. You know how she feels about that." Tammy's older brother, Mike, had been killed in Khe Sanh in 1968, when she was sixteen. There was a photograph of a smiling Uncle Mike that hung on the mantel. In the picture he was drinking a Budweiser and leaning on a Huey helicopter. Looking at the picture, Tim had wondered on more than one occasion if there wasn't some version of Uncle Mike in some parallel universe who hadn't gotten killed.

"I know. I won't." Tim thought about asking a question about Uncle Mike, steal some cool factoid about his ever-smiling mystery uncle, but decided to change the subject instead. "How much longer do you think the patio is going to take?"

"It's still June, right?"

"Yep."

"Longer than June."

"I'll get a shovel," said Tim as he stood to walk around the house. He couldn't see it, but behind him, his dad was smiling.

———

The gravel seemed almost magical: no matter how much of it Tim and his dad moved, the pile always seemed to be the same size. Tim mentioned this to his dad, saying that he was pretty sure they were stuck in a time warp. His dad didn't respond, and Tim took that as an agreement that yes, they had been abducted by some alien entity that loved to watch men move wheelbarrows full of stone. Finally, after about an hour and six loads of pea gravel, Tim's mother stuck her head out the front door of their ranch-style house with an announcement that dinner was done.

"All right," said Stan. "We'll be right in. Go wash up, buckaroo. I'll dump this last load."

Tim did not need to be told twice. He put the shovel back in the vertical rack where the yard tools were kept, then ran inside to wash his hands in the kitchen sink. It was hot in the house. Bearable due to a brilliantly devised series of fans set up by his mom every year, but still hot. Tim walked through the kitchen and sat at the dining room table, across from a furious-looking Becca.

"What's shakin', Bacon?" Tim asked his sister, who stole a glance at their mom in the kitchen, saw that she was busy doing something, and flipped her younger brother the bird. Bacon was an old nickname for Becca; a very young Tim had called her Beccan for several months, and their parents had found it hilarious. Becca had too, until a few months ago. Now, Tim said it either to annoy her or as a genuine mistake of habit.

A few moments later Stan entered the kitchen, washed his hands, and sat at the table with his children. Tammy was close behind, with an enormous bowl of salad.

"I don't want to hear it," she said as she set the bowl down in the center of the table. "It's too hot to cook anything in here, and until that patio's done, your father can't grill. There's some incentive for you, Stan. As soon as it's done we can have some steaks."

"And if I say I like salad and no longer want to grill, thus meaning I no longer require a patio, can we leave it as is?" He said this slowly, stealing looks at his children. Becca was even smiling, despite herself.

"Trust me, Stanley," Tammy said just as slowly, but with a wicked smile, "you want to have a patio. Especially now that you've started. Besides, I saw you and Tim working out there—you're at least halfway done."

"Half of half, maybe," said Stan, piling his plate high with Caesar salad. "There's still a long way to go."

"Dad, can I go to a movie?" Becca asked in a sweet voice, but before he could answer, Mom broke in: "I said you may ask your father after dinner."

"What movie?" he asked.

"Why does that matter?"

Tim's eyes were already darting between the participants of what was likely to be a violent but short-lived skirmish.

"Tell him," said Tammy. "Then tell him who else is going." She was smiling again, even more evilly, Tim noted, than when Dad had jokingly suggested that the patio project go on hiatus.

"*Full Metal Jacket* and *The Untouchables*, at the drive-in," Becca sighed, eyes focused on her still-empty plate. "And a bunch of people are going. Jammi, Molly, Tara, Tracy, Stacey—lots of people. It's going to be cool."

"Tell him who else," cooed Tammy, between bites of salad. "Because as much as I hate the idea of you seeing a couple of R-rated movies with all of your polite, well-mannered, and utterly gracious girlfriends, all of whom I'm sure are saving themselves for marriage, I really love the idea of that deadbeat—"

"He is not a deadbeat!" Becca nearly shouted. "Tyler is cool, and didn't even ask me to go. He's just going to be there, it's not like it's a date or anything."

"Which is good," snapped Tammy. Tim forced himself not to smile as he ate. "Because as it has been made quite clear to you on numerous occasions, you are not going to be dating anyone. Not Tyler Cranston, not Harrison Ford, not anybody."

"Heard some great news, Mom," snapped Becca in an exact replica of her mom's tone. "It is now the 1980s, and *everyone* is dating. Even babies like Tim go on dates if they're not too ugly, or busy playing with their loser buddies."

"Twelve-year-olds are dating?" Tim asked. That was news to him.

His question was ignored, however, as his dad stood, dumped salad on his daughter's plate, and sat back down. "Becca, eat." To demonstrate, he stuffed a forkful of salad between his lips, chewed, and continued. "And she did say it wasn't a date, Tam."

Tammy rolled her eyes at her husband, who pretended not to notice. "So if it's not a date, what is it?"

"A gathering of friends," said Becca, her voice all but dead.

"And will this gathering of friends be consuming alcohol or smoking pot?"

Becca rolled her eyes. "None of my friends do that. They're not idiots. Besides, Tyler has to stay away from all that stuff, or he could lose eligibility for football. Even the people that do that stuff don't do it around him, just because it wouldn't be fair for him to lose his chance at a letter."

"When would you be arriving home?" Stan asked.

"When the second movie is done."

Stan Benchley made the sound of a buzzer going off. "Not good enough," he said, pointing at a clock that was hanging on the wall over Becca's head. "Those run on hours and minutes, not movies. When does this all start?"

"Seven thirty."

"Who's driving?"

"Jammi."

"She has her license?"

"Got held back in first grade because she needed glasses and they didn't figure it out until too late." Becca chuckled into her fist. "They thought she was retarded."

"All right," said Stan, between bites. "Mom gets last approval on clothing and makeup; you're home not one second after my clock, not yours, says midnight; and you make good choices. You were raised right. Don't make me into a bad guy for letting you do something a little grown up."

Becca shrieked, and Tim watched his dad ignore a positively evil look from his mom. "Thanks, Daddy, I'll be good, I promise."

"You better be," said Tammy somberly. "I feel like having wine. Tim, would you do me the honor?"

"*Oui, madame.*" Tim jumped out of his chair and headed for the pantry. He had been taught how to work a corkscrew only a few months ago. *Sweet.*

3

Hooper sang as he showered. He started—loudly—with the national anthem, and then switched it up to the theme from *Cheers*. He had a good singing voice, but it wasn't something that anyone knew about, because it was something he was almost, but not quite, embarrassed of. The water slowly began to turn from hot to cold, and Hooper shut it off, then stood in the shower to enjoy a final moment of warmth from the steam. It was good to be clean. He stepped out of the shower, grabbed a towel, and quickly ran it over his body. Not as taut as it had been in the shit back in the day, but still, not terrible.

Once he was mostly dry, Hooper walked naked to the bedroom, giving himself a look in the mirror, and feeling a stirring in his loins at the sight. *I look good.* Looking good was important, that was what women liked, and being liked by women was very important. Having a sense of humor was good too, but Hooper had never felt very confident in that aspect of his personality, almost like he had to force himself to even fake being funny, and still wasn't very good at it. Still, the kind of woman Hooper liked was the kind you paid to have a good time, and Hooper figured that if they had to pretend to laugh at his jokes, it was still lucky for them to be with such a good-looking guy. His mom had always said he would grow up to be a handsome man, and she was right.

Hooper got dressed slowly—bright blue briefs, a tight black T-shirt, and jeans. He slid on a pair of cowboy boots, no socks, and then pushed a snub-nosed .38 into his pants pocket. He practiced drawing the gun a few times, sliding it in and out of his jeans to make sure it wouldn't get hung up on anything if he needed it quickly. It passed the test well, as he'd figured it would. He'd had the hammer bobbed a few years back, and had replaced the factory rubber grip with a smooth faux-pearl one. The grips made the revolver almost too slick, especially when shooting, but Hooper didn't figure he'd need to do any shooting tonight. Usually the knife, a KA-BAR just like he'd had in Nam, was enough, if it came to that. He slid the sheathed blade into his boot, and did a little dance as he left the bedroom.

Hooper walked into the kitchen and poured himself a glass of milk from the half gallon in the fridge. He drank it quickly, then placed the glass in the sink and rinsed it out; the last thing he needed was flies. Hooper kept the house immaculately clean, everything in its place. It was how his mom had raised him, and since this was her old house, it was only fair to honor her memory by keeping it the way it had been when she was alive. Hooper checked his watch. It would be dark soon, and time to leave.

Hooper walked from the kitchen, thinking, like he always did, about Amy, his little sister. She'd disappeared when he was in Vietnam, when she was just sixteen years old. He had some theories about where she might have gone, and why she would have left, but he really wanted to ask her himself, find out why she'd wanted to do something so hard on their mom. It just wasn't a fair thing to do. Hooper could remember Amy like it was yesterday. He'd slowly watched her develop, and he could remember the smell of her hair like his nose was buried in it right now.

There were a lot of girls out there who looked like Amy, but Hooper was pretty particular. Usually, he'd cruise up and down

Division Avenue, heading south and looking at all of the working girls. It was normal not to see a girl who looked like her, and on those nights, Hooper would pick one of the other girls and fuck her in his car, then drive her to where she asked him to. Those girls never saw the pistol, or the knife. The Amy look-alikes got a different sort of treatment. Hooper liked to rape them at knifepoint, sometimes at the drive-in, sometimes other places on the north end of town—he wasn't too particular about that part. While he raped the Amys, he always asked why they had left, and if they knew how much they'd hurt Mom. None of them ever knew the answer to either question.

When he was done, he drove the women to Riverside Park. Usually, by about that point he would start to realize just how much they didn't look like Amy, how they couldn't possibly be Amy. By the time he would get to the park he would be furious, and the usual pathetic crying didn't help at all. Hooper had done the same thing fourteen times, finishing by stabbing the fake Amy once through the liver with the KA-BAR, and then choking them into silence. The bodies were found by the police, and usually made the news. No one was looking too hard—after all, they were just prostitutes, street trash not worth much more than a dog or a cat. Hooper smiled. He probably wouldn't find Amy tonight, but he could sure as hell go looking, and have a nice time either way.

4

Scott's mom had to work late on Mondays, so he and his stepdad, Carl, ate cold leftover pizza from the fridge, neither of them speaking as the meal was slowly consumed. The TV spoke for them. The news was on, and once again, the talking heads were arguing over whether or not the United States should retaliate further against Iraq for its missile attack on the USS *Stark* in May. Thirty-seven sailors had been killed, and apparently that was enough for the 'nuclear' word to be used.

"They should do it," said Carl. "Fuck it. Turn the goddamn desert to glass, then send a couple up for the gooks and Russians. Get this Cold War hot, and let God figure it out."

Scott knew better than to refute his stepdad, or to even bother trying to argue an alternative viewpoint. Carl Andrews had been living with them since Scott was six, two years after Scott's dad had boarded his pickup truck, gone to work, and never come back. Scott had received a Christmas card a few years later, but he had just thrown it away. Though he wasn't the biggest Carl fan, Carl was around, and was promising to take him deer hunting for the first time when Scott turned sixteen. Besides, Scott figured his mother, Beth, could do worse than the Vietnam vet, who was currently employed as a tool-and-die engineer on the south end of town. He rarely drank, never to excess, and Scott's mom at least seemed happy with him. Still, having a dad who just up and left one day can leave a hell of a mark, and Scott could still feel the sting of it.

"Why don't you get off your butt," said Carl, making Scott jump, "see if the Tigs are on yet. I've had enough of this depressing crap. Reminds me way too much of the buildup to Nam. At least we finally did something there, when they let us, that is."

"Was it scary?"

The question fell out of Scott's mouth accidentally. He had long wanted to talk to his stepdad about the conflict that still seemed visible in the national rearview mirror, but had never done so, and was terrified at the prospect of what the man might say. Now, with his mother gone and the Tigers tied 0–0 at the top of the second inning, the sound of a pin dropping would have been thermonuclear in the silence.

"Yeah," said Carl. "And anybody that would tell you otherwise is an idiot. But there were good parts too. Knowing that if you did your job right your buddies would live, and if they did theirs, you might too.

"The worst part was all the traps Charlie would build. Not just land mines—those were scary as hell too, of course, but I mean other stuff. Like, they'd sharpen a bunch of sticks, rub shit all over them, and then dig a hole. You step in that and it goes through your boot, you'll be lucky if you don't lose the leg. It was scary, but it wasn't all scary. I made some of my best friends in that war. Like Hooper. That was where we hooked up. You remember him?"

Scott was not a fan of Hooper. He'd been over a few times to help work on Scott's mom's troubled Oldsmobile, and had seemed to spend a lot more time fondling tools and ogling his mother than he had fixing the car. She had pretended not to notice, Scott could tell, and Carl either didn't care or didn't notice.

"Yeah, he helped you fix the car."

"Right, when the tranny went. Jesus, you see that? One–nothing. Sheridan just came home, good start. Anyways, yeah, it was scary, real scary. But despite what all those fucking hippies said at the time, and all the antiwar people say now, it wasn't all bad. They don't know what it was like to be hunting other men, and let me tell you, it beats the shit out of sitting under a tree and shooting a buck. And I like shooting a buck a whole hell of a lot. That's the thing none of your teachers are going to tell you, and none of the books you read, even the ones that tell the truth, are going to have printed in them. Some people are built for war, and for the ones who are, there is nothing more satisfying than being good at it. Like when you beat the snot out of that kid last fall—"

"Mike Haverford. He pushed a girl down."

"Yeah, that asshole. You felt pretty damn good afterward, right?"

"Yeah." Scott blushed at the memory. Alice Klein had kissed him after his suspension was up.

"Well, war can be like that. It can be scary, and awful when one of your buddies gets hurt, but it can be great too. When that napalm would roll in and we could feel those assholes roasting like pork chops, man. Look at that, Brookens just got two in, a double. Three–nothing, Tigs." Carl stood. "Get these dishes cleaned up, and then come watch the game with me. They might be finally turning that losing streak around."

5

Luke Hutchinson sat watching the Tigers while his mother sat smoking and talking on the phone to a friend. Unlike Scott and Tim, Luke didn't live in the suburbs on the other side of the forest. He lived in a trailer park called the Cruise Inn, which was a fairly odd name, as most who came seemed to stay. Luke knew that he, his mom, and his younger twin sisters didn't have as much money as a lot of the other kids that he hung around with, but it didn't matter, at least not to him. The trailer park existed to allow lower-income people to still have their kids in the well-regarded Northview Public School system. The majority of kids who attended those schools were suburban children of baby boomers, but there were kids from two other trailer parks too, along with those from a pair of cheap apartment complexes.

The division between these less-well-off children and their better-heeled fellows in the suburbs was less marked than one would have expected in their quiet North Kent County school district. Luke had thought about that a few times, not that he'd ever mentioned it to Tim or Scott. His theory was that while there were some kids at Northview whose families had money, *real money*, there were very few of them. And because there were so few, it was almost more awkward for those kids than for the poor kids. A couple years earlier, Luke had gone to an acquaintance's to hang out, a boy named Jeff Baker. Luke didn't realize just how well-off Jeff was until they arrived at his house. It was huge! Pool, indoor hot tub, all the kids had their own rooms and bathrooms—it was easily the nicest house Luke had ever been in. Even still, what he remembered most from the visit was Jeff asking him, almost begging him, not to tell anyone else about the house. After that, Luke just figured that different was different, and no kid wants to be the weird one, no matter what the reason is.

Lately, Luke had felt a bit like the weird kid, even if he wasn't sharing that with his best friends. His mom, even though he loved her very much, seemed to be spiraling out of control. She was smoking more than ever, and drinking too, sometimes in the morning and at night. She had trouble keeping a job for more than a few months at a time, and the family they'd been before she kicked Luke's dad out was a lot different than it was now. Back when he worked at Case, they were always one step from making it. Now they were always just a few feet from the gutter.

Luke never told anyone about his plans for the future, not his mom, not his friends, and certainly not that annoying guidance counselor at school. His friends loved all the cool war stuff he was always reading about and sharing with them, but what they didn't know was why he read it in the first place. Luke planned to enlist on his eighteenth birthday, rain or shine. He figured it was as good a way out as any, and a hell of a lot more to count on than to hope for a scholarship. He wanted out of the park, out of his mother's house, even away from his annoying little sisters. As for them, Luke felt that Ashley and Alisha were inevitably destined to appear on one of those trashy daytime talk shows his mom watched sometimes, where they showed kids and people who had made royal fuck-jobs of their lives. Granted, the twins were only eleven, but both already had a reputation, and those tended to grow as one got older, and usually were pretty accurate.

The Tigers game let him ignore his sisters bickering in their room, his mom blabbing on the phone with a Camel hanging out of her mouth, and all the other nonsense around him. Anyone looking at him would have thought that the kid he or she saw was entranced by the shellacking the Tigers were putting on the Milwaukee Brewers, 10–0 in the bottom of the fifth. He or she never would have known that, while Luke may have been there, in his mind he was crawling through a rice paddy, readying himself to make a thousand-yard shot on a female sniper known as Apache, who had been torturing captured US soldiers. The story played out in his mind as he finally dragged himself off of the couch, brushed his teeth, and went to his room. His mom was still on the phone and his sisters still arguing as Luke lay in bed, trying his best to ignore them all, and to make his one shot count.

6

Tim woke in his bed, sure that he was still dreaming. The hall lights were turned on, and there was shouting coming from the living room. He could hear Becca and both of his parents. *Home late*, thought Tim devilishly, and then he looked at his clock and saw that it was only 11:38. Still Monday night. Curious, and unable to help himself, he leapt from his bed and began plodding from his room toward the noise. He caught only snippets of conversation, and was able to understand none of it, until he made the hall. Then quite clearly, he heard his dad say, "I'm going to fucking kill him," just as he walked in.

They stopped talking. Becca had makeup running down her face, way more than their mom ever would have approved of, and she was wearing clothing he didn't recognize. The outfit didn't look like it would have garnered a positive response either, but most troubling about it was the tear in the low collar of her shirt. Dad looked pissed, madder than Tim could remember ever seeing him, even more than that time Tim spilled all that paint in the driveway. Mom looked really sad—scary sad, just like Becca did.

"Stanley, you get Tim back to bed," Tammy said. "This will still be waiting when you come back. And calm down. No more yelling, not from anybody, OK?" Dad didn't say anything to her, just walked to Tim, pointed to the hallway, and walked behind him back to his room. Tim hopped back into bed, and his dad sat on the floor next to it. He didn't look mad anymore. He looked worse, like maybe he wanted to hurt somebody, maybe even kill them. Tim was used to his dad with his nose in a book, grading papers, or lately, looking sadly at the hole in the backyard. This was very different.

"How much did you hear?" Stan asked, finally. His voice was flat, like the life had been sucked out of him.

"I don't know. Mostly just a bunch of noise, and then you said the *F* word, and that you were going to kill someone. What happened to Becca?"

"I'm not sure yet," said Stan. "Not exactly, in any case. If I had to guess, a boy, probably that Tyler kid, got a little fresh with your sister, and she told him to dial it back a notch. When he didn't…well, I'm not sure what exactly happened. I suppose I'll know soon enough."

"So are you going to kill him?"

"No. No, I don't think so. This is probably one of those things that can be handled a little differently than that." He smiled. "I'm not sure I'd be much good at killing, after all. I'd likely bungle it all up, end up not killing anybody, and going to jail to boot. I don't think it's in my genes. I suppose that's a good thing."

"So what are you going to do?"

"I don't know, buddy. I really don't. But you don't need to worry about any of this silly stuff, at least not for a few more years at least."

"I'm not sure I want to get any older."

"I don't either," said Stan, almost chuckling. "You get some winks, Tim, and don't worry about Becca. She'll be fine, all right?"

"If you say so."

7

Detective Dick Van Endel woke to the twin sounds of his pager and the phone ringing. He checked the clock: 2:37 a.m. *Christ.* Ignoring the pager, he yawned, gave the mostly empty glass of whiskey on the nightstand an ugly look, and answered the phone. There was a pause, and then a click.

"Van Endel."

"Jesus, Dick. Where are you?" It was his partner, Phil Nelson. His nickname had been Full Nelson until he'd lost thirty pounds and threatened to beat the shit out of the next man who used that term to describe anything besides a headlock.

"I'm at home," Van Endel said. "I take it I need to answer that page on the double?"

"Yes, please do. They're driving me nuts. Plus, I think Sarah is going to kill me if I leave her alone with all the fucking machines again. For fuck's sake, they know I'm on leave. Why are they even calling me?"

Phil's wife, Sarah, was pregnant, about six months along, and things weren't going well. They had her on bed rest, and evidently had her hooked up to twenty-seven different machines to monitor her condition. Phil was on emergency leave until they successfully got the kid out of her. Phil and Van Endel had joked just two days earlier that something terrible was going to happen while Phil was gone, perhaps another dead whore at Riverside, maybe something worse. As Van Endel listened to his pager wail, the joking was an ugly memory.

"Well, sorry they had to bug you, Phil. Give Sarah my love, all right? And don't let this stress you out. We talked about that. I got shit under control, no matter how thick it may get."

"Thanks, buddy. Make me proud." Phil hung up, and Van Endel depressed the button to make his end click off, then released it again. He grabbed the pager, then punched in the number.

"This is Dispatch," said the female operator on the other end.

"Van Endel, returning a page. Whaddya got?"

"Possible 207, sixteen-year-old girl. A couple of uniforms on the scene already. They requested you."

Van Endel gritted his teeth. That wasn't good. Usually, a possible 207 on a kid that old took a few days to process. There had to be a part of the story he wasn't getting yet. Van Endel took a pen and a tattered Moleskine from his nightstand. "Got an address for me?"

She rattled it off quickly. Once he had all the details—apartment on the north end, single mother named Samantha Peterson, missing girl named Molly Peterson—he thanked her and hung up the phone.

Van Endel briefly considered a shower to remove his whiskey-sweat, but decided on cologne instead. He dressed in a black suit that was as comfortable as his favorite pair of pajamas but still looked reasonably sharp, then ran a comb through his hair. Given what he'd thrown down before he'd dozed off (he preferred that to "passed out"), he knew he had no right to look as good as he did. He hoisted a smile at the mirror to see if he could carry it off. He supposed he could. And then, just that quick, thoughts of her, of Lex, took the smile off of his face. He left the mirror behind, threw on his shoulder holster, tucked his wallet into the rear right pocket of his pants, and shrugged on his jacket. It was going to be a long night, and probably a long day, but that was OK. This work was everything that he was.

There were two marked cars parked at the apartment complex, and Van Endel parked his Chevy Caprice behind them before getting out. He gave his notes a look for the address, then saw a uniform he recognized, Don Pratt, standing by a door across the lot. Van Endel opened the door and climbed from the car, then closed the door quietly, before rubbing his palms together and walking to the uni. Waking up was hard to do. "How's it shaking, Donny?"

"Mrs. Peterson is inside losing her shit, Dick. Just so you know. And thanks for asking. I've been good. My kids are at summer camp all week, and I plan on fucking my wife every chance I get until they get back."

"This must be throwing a monkey wrench in that plan," said Van Endel, grinning. "We'll get you back to it soon."

"Hey, no sweat on my end," said Don. "I had to work tonight either way, may as well be doing something. You talk to Phil?"

"Yeah, briefly. I didn't get a progress report or anything, though. I just know that Sarah's in a holding pattern. What's your take on our missing kid?" He eyed the Petersons' door.

"Kid's gone," said Don. "Aside from that, tough to tell you. Mom thinks they were at the drive-in, but Molly never came home. Sorry, missing girl's name is Molly, not sure if you had that. In any case, Mrs. Peterson called it in, and we were here a little later. Once we figured out that Mrs. Peterson most likely was not full of shit, I put in for a detective. Hope you don't have plans."

"Only plan I had was sleeping one off," said Van Endel. "I'm going to go talk to the missus, you call me once your week in paradise is over, we'll hit the Shipwreck and get a beer."

"That sounds great, Dick. I'll keep you posted."

On his way into the apartment building, Van Endel walked into the doorframe, hard, with his shoulder. *Take a deep breath, you're doing fine.* Willing the booze away wasn't going to happen, but he could at least ignore it. Feeling a bit more together now—the bump with the frame might have been a good thing—Van Endel saw another uniform at the top of the steps, this one a woman he didn't recognize. He walked to her, showed her his badge, and she opened the door for him.

The apartment smelled like cigarettes and had amateurish paintings hanging on the walls. Van Endel stopped briefly to look at one—it was signed *MP* and was of a sunset—then stepped into the kitchen. Mrs. Peterson was sitting at a table, smoking a cigarette, and talking to a uniform. But the talking stopped when they saw Van Endel.

"Mrs. Peterson?" he asked, and she nodded. Van Endel extended a hand that she shook with her own cold and clammy hand, her fingers small and thin. "May I have a seat?"

"Of course, and please, call me Sam."

Van Endel sat and nodded to the uniform at the table, a vet named Walt Summers. Walt and Dick had been to a few of these over the last couple of years, late-night calls that never seemed to turn out how anyone wanted, and almost always found their end in the expansive lawns of Riverside Park.

"It's a pleasure to meet you, Mrs. Peterson, though I can't help but imagine we could do so under better circumstances. I'm Detective Richard Van Endel, Dick for short. I want you to tell me everything that you can recall about your daughter's plans this evening. I know you've probably already done this, but please humor me. I want your daughter home safe and in bed almost as badly as you do."

"She went to the drive-in with her friends," said Sam. "I was sort of on the fence about letting her go, but…Do you have kids, Detective?" Van Endel shook his head. "Well, Officer Summers here and I were just talking about how it's all about balance with raising children, especially a free spirit like Molly. If you don't let them do some of the stuff that you don't want them to do, then they're going to do *all* the stuff you don't want them to, only it'll be behind your back."

He nodded. "Makes sense. What kind of stuff are we talking about, if I may ask?"

"Oh, nothing awful," she said. "Boys. Molly likes to play the wild thing, but I know she's not. Not really." She smiled. "A parent's greatest asset can be making your child forget that you're not an authority figure, but a friend. You still *are* a parent, of course, but especially raising a girl alone, it's good that she can tell me things I don't want to hear. It's how I know she's OK. Does that make sense?"

"It does," said Van Endel, who was wondering, and not for the first time, if he would ever have children. The chances seemed remote at this point. Nights like this, he was OK with it. "What time did she leave?"

"Just after seven. Her friend Jammi Walther drove them, they were meeting some other friends there." She took a long drag from her cigarette, then continued. "Rebecca Benchley was in the car as well. Could have been someone else too, for all I know.

"Here's the thing. Molly had a strict curfew, and she knew it. I don't worry much about what she does when she's out—she's got common sense and tells me everything about her life—but the curfew is something she knows she has to respect. That was why I called. She's never late, not ever. I didn't want to be one of those crazy people calling her friends, but I finally snapped and called Jammi's mom, since Jammi drove."

"What did they have to say?"

"That Jammi saw Molly necking with some boy, and then they were just gone. There was a big scuffle between one of the other girls and a boy—Becca, I think—and then all the teenagers were clearing out of there. That was why I called. All the other kids were home on time, and they saw my daughter go off with some boy that no one knew, and no one could call me?"

"Sam, you need to relax," said Van Endel, reaching across the table to take one of her forearms in his hand. "Molly has only been gone a few hours. You need to get some rest, take a Valium if you have some, and in the morning, call all of her friends. That is, if she doesn't come home in between, of course." He smiled thinly. "Kids, good kids even, do stupid, disrespectful things all the time. Hopefully this turns out to be nothing more than a family problem."

"Then why are there so many police in my home, Detective?" Sam asked bitterly. "If everything is still OK, why is it so far past curfew and my daughter isn't home? I read the papers. I know all about the bodies at Riverside—"

"Mrs. Peterson," said Van Endel, interrupting her and raising a hand. "Those girls are not like your daughter. They were all known prostitutes, and they were all taken miles from that drive-in. Molly was nowhere close to that area, and there's no reason to be drawing that conclusion." He took a card from his pocket with his name and contact information on it, and slid it across the table to her. "This phone number goes directly to my desk. Get some sleep—just read a book and relax if you can't—and then call me in the morning, either way." He stood. "I hope to hear in the morning that she's home."

"You won't," said Sam, as she lit another cigarette. "Like I said, she respects a curfew, and this isn't how she is."

8

When Tim woke Tuesday morning, he stripped off his pajamas and quickly dressed. Next, he brushed his teeth and headed off to the kitchen, not totally sure that the events of the night before had actually taken place. Everything sure seemed like a dream, but when he got to the kitchen, he knew it wasn't. His dad was nowhere to be found, but his mom and Becca were sitting at the table. His mom looked angry now, instead of sad like before, and Becca looked miserable.

Ignoring them, or at least trying to, Tim filled a bowl with Cheerios, topped them with milk, then grabbed a spoon and sat at the table. "What's going on?" he asked.

Becca stood. "I'm going to my room." She stomped off, looking tired, furious, and indignant all at the same time.

Tammy called after her, "We're not done talking about this, young lady!"

A door slammed in the distance in answer. Tammy took a slow drink of coffee and then set the mug on the table before turning to look at her son.

"Your sister made some questionable choices," she said. "As did some of her friends, and some boys made those bad decisions almost turn out a whole lot worse."

"Tyler Cranston?"

"No," Tammy said, frowning. "At least I don't think so. Becca hasn't told me exactly who it was, just that they met some older guys and things didn't go as planned."

"Dad said he wasn't really going to kill anybody."

"Good. I'm not sure your father has that in him. Which is a good thing, Tim. My brother—your uncle Mike—he thought he was a pretty rough guy, and he signed up for the army along with a bunch of other guys who thought they were too, and a whole lot of them came back in boxes.

"There's nothing wrong with just being a regular guy like Dad. In fact, it's a really good thing. There's also nothing wrong with being a gentleman, unlike those guys your sister met. Do you know what I mean when I say that? If you want, I can get Dad and you two can talk a—"

The ringing phone cut her off, but as she moved to stand, it stopped. She waited for Becca to yell that it was for one of them, and when she didn't Tammy opened her mouth to continue. Seeing an opening, Tim cut her off.

"I know what you mean," said Tim, having no idea what she meant at all. "I don't need to talk to Dad about it either. Besides, he's probably really busy."

Tammy turned, leaning back in her chair to look out of the blinds into the backyard. She had excellent timing: as she turned, Stan heaved a transfer shovel to the ground in disgust. "You may be on to something, Tim. Your father does seem to have his hands full." A sad smile pulled at her lips, but then gave up. She looked at him. "But if you want to talk about this, we can. Just give your sister some space, and try and be nice without being obvious about it.

"Oh, and one more thing: this is a problem *our* family has, and it does not need to be blabbed all over the neighborhood. Becca has a reputation to think of. Is that clear?"

"Yes, Mom." Both of them turned as Becca came back into the room, and Tim forced an insincere smile onto his face.

Ignoring him, Becca said, "That was Molly's mom. Molly never came home last night."

"Is she still on the phone?" Tammy asked as she stood, walking quickly to the kitchen phone. "Did you tell her what happened?"

"No, Mom. I'm sure she's fine." Tammy, who was dialing before Becca could finish talking, stuck the phone to her ear and said, "Tim, find something to do outside."

9

When Hooper had first seen her, he'd nearly crashed his car. Once he'd wrapped his head around what he'd just seen, he circled back to pull up in front of her. She approached the car with caution, not like the normal streetwalkers he was used to dealing with, who were so hard up for drugs that their nerves and good sense had been fried. She leaned in the car and said, "I've got a room a few blocks from here. You want to go party?" The way she said it was unsure and nervous, but it was also perfect, she was new to the streets. She also resembled Amy more than any girl he'd ever seen before; it was almost impossible that they could look so similar.

"Sounds good," he said, and as she slid into the car next to him, he slipped the revolver from his pocket.

"I'm staying a couple blocks south at the—"

Hooper cut her off, raising the revolver as he spoke. "You're going to shut up right now," he said, the words coming out of some other him that always knew exactly what to say and do in these situations. "If you just sit back and relax, you're going to be just fine. OK, sweetheart?"

She nodded, her eyes big and focused on the shiny handgun. *She wants me.* Hooper could tell she did, because even with the terror in her eyes he could see lust shining through.

"You're new out here, aren't you, Amy?" Hooper asked, and the girl nodded in response. "That's good," he said. "These streets are no place for a girl as pretty as you. You should be at home with your mom and dad, not out here. Did your dad get a little touchy-feely, make you want to take off? I get that. Happens all the time. But this is your lucky day. I'm going to take you away from all of this."

"Please let me go," said the girl. "My name's not Amy, it's Molly. You've got me confused with someone else. Just let me go, I won't tell anyone. I'm not supposed to be out here. I just want to go home."

Hooper smiled. She'd be begging to be called Amy soon enough. He was nicer to Amy. "Where are you supposed to be instead, honey?"

"We were going to the drive-in. This was all supposed to be just a gag or something, just for fun. Just drop me off right here, OK? Just stop and let me out."

Hooper raised the gun and pointed it at her. He hated doing it. *God, she looks just like her.* "Get your hand off of the car door. Now. Do it slowly, and put your hands in your lap like a good girl." She did it as he watched, just like he'd told her to. They were almost to the park, just a few more blocks, and he was going to have her.

Out of nowhere, another thought occurred to him: What if, instead of using her and then disposing of her, he saved her? She was as close to Amy at sixteen as he was ever going to get, even if he found his real sister. Instead of turning left, Hooper turned right, sending them away from the park.

Hooper smiled at the silently crying girl, already becoming resigned to her fate, thanks to the pistol. *If I'm going to do this, it has to be perfect.* "You said you were going to the drive-in, right?"

She ignored him, and Hooper asked again. "Amy, you said you were going to the drive-in, right?"

"Yes," she said in a very small voice. "But now I just want to go home. Can you please just let me go home?"

Hooper smiled at her. Even with the makeup running down her face, she was beautiful. "Of course you can go home, Amy. In fact, that's exactly where we're headed. Now, your room isn't quite like what it was when you left, but we should be able to get it fixed up soon enough, all right?"

"Just let me go!" she screamed, banging her hands on the dashboard. For a moment Hooper thought he might have to hit her with the gun just to make her behave. That would ruin it, though, mess up that pretty face. She just needed the proper training and everything would be fine.

"Amy, if I have to ask you to calm down again, I'm going to be forced to hurt you, and that's the last thing I want to do." Her screaming turned into bawling, and Hooper ran his gun hand through her hair. *Just like Amy.*

———

Hooper parked the car in the garage. He had never planned to bring one of them here, and wasn't exactly sure what to do. He got out of the car and walked around it, then opened her door, grabbed the girl by the arm, and yanked her out. She opened her mouth to scream, he knew she was going to, and he dropped the hand holding the pistol on top of her head. He caught her body before she could fall to the floor, and was surprised at how little she weighed. Hooper kicked the car door shut, then carried her into the house.

He walked through the kitchen with her and laid her down on the couch. He tucked the pistol into his pants and ran back to the garage. There was some nautical rope in his toolbox, he was almost positive. The rope was in the third drawer he checked, and

Hooper grabbed it, along with a box cutter, and raced back in through the kitchen to the living room. He let out a deep breath. She was still on the couch. He sat down next to her and began using the rope to bind her hands and feet.

When he was done, she was stripped to her underwear, her ankles were bound, and her wrists were tied behind her back. Hooper had used additional rope to attach her ankles to her wrists to create a higher level of security. He checked his watch. It was only 11:00 p.m., so if he hurried, he had enough time to make everything else happen. He hoisted up the now-bound Amy and carried her down to the cellar, along with the rope and box cutter. Once there, he laid her back against a steel beam wrapped in cement, then tied her restraints to the pole using the rest of the rope. He gave it a good yank, and when he was sure that she wouldn't be getting loose, he grabbed the box cutter and stood, giving her one long last look before climbing the steps and locking the basement door.

He needed to hurry to Meijer to get supplies, and then he needed to go back to Division Street to get another girl, someone who at the very least was a size similar to Amy. Everything was happening so fast, but Hooper knew it was as it was supposed to be. Amy was finally home. Now he just had to do everything right so she could stay there for a very long time.

10

Scott and Luke were already in the fort when Tim got there. He could tell even before he began to ascend the ladder, before he could hear them talking or try to see through the windows. That was because when the boys had first built the fort, they'd installed a security system, so that they would know if a stranger was up there waiting for them. The idea had been Scott's stepdad's on his lone trip to see the thing, and it was simple: All three boys were to keep a bottle cap in their pants pocket at all times. Scott had Coke, Tim had Budweiser, and Luke had Sprite. If they came alone, they were always to check at the base of the ladder that was farthest north, or closest to Tim's house. No caps placed on the ground under the bottom rung, but noise coming from upstairs? That meant run home and get an adult.

Today, Tim saw the Coke and Sprite caps right where they were supposed to be, and he flipped his Budweiser cap next to them out of habit, just as Scott's stepdad had told them to. "You have to do it every time," he'd said, "or it'll be pointless and you could end up getting killed by some drifter anyway." The boys had nodded at this passing of valuable knowledge, and all of them loved the ritual that felt almost like something James Bond would do.

His cap in place, Tim slowly began to ascend the ladder. All three of them could do it quickly—Scott the fastest by far—but it was still pretty cool to go slowly and look at how the forest changed as you climbed. There was nothing out of the ordinary to see—the boys' near-constant presence in the woods would've sent most local wildlife in search of a quieter locale—but there was still a lot to take in. Even the trees looked cooler the higher up Tim got, and no matter how many times he did it, the trip to the top never seemed to get boring.

Tim arose from the hole in the floor, then transitioned from the last rungs of the ladder to the waiting safety of the fort. Luke grabbed his forearm as he came over the gap in the wood, and then Tim felt the faint sense of vertigo fade. Feet planted on semi-solid ground, Tim thanked Luke for the hand and asked the other boys what they were doing.

"Nothing," said Luke. "Just trying to hit that target again, or at least we were."

"Yeah," said Scott dejectedly. "Either our guns suck, or we suck. Probably both."

"Well, we're not going to get better guns," said Tim. "I had to bug my mom forever just to let me get this one. There's no way she's going to let me get a better one, not even if I got a paper route and saved my own money."

"Good luck getting a paper route around here," said Luke. "The Bennetts have that locked up until they die." This was an endlessly sore point for any cash-strapped neighborhood child old enough to have a bicycle. The Bennett brothers, a pair of alcoholics who lived in Luke's trailer park, had miles' and miles' worth of paper routes, and had used them as a sole source of income for as long as anyone could remember. The worst part was that the Bennett brothers, drunks or not, did a great job with their thousands of deliveries and there was no way they were going to get fired anytime soon.

"Yeah," said Tim. "I know. It just sucks, is all. I know my dad would let me get a better gun, maybe even a .22 like I fired one time up north, but my mom won't have a real gun in the house."

"Hey, did you guys hear about Molly Peterson?" Scott said, changing the subject. "Her mom and my mom are friends at work, and I guess Molly never came home last night. My mom said that, knowing Molly, she wouldn't be surprised if she was shacked up with a sailor or something for a few days, but I guess her mom is totally freaking out."

"I heard about that," said Tim. "Her mom called my mom this morning. Molly was out to the movies last night with my sister and…" Tim trailed off.

"And what?" Luke asked him. "What happened at the movies?"

"Well," said Tim, "the thing is, I don't know exactly. Also, my mom told me not to tell anyone about it. She said it was private family stuff, and that it was supposed to stay that way."

"Hey," said Scott, "we're not just friends, we're blood brothers, remember?"

Tim did. The three had sealed a pact in blood coaxed from their pinkies three years prior. Scott had a point, but Tim's mother's words still rang in his head. "Yeah, I know," he said. "But my mom was super serious about not telling anyone about what happened to Becca. She said it could be bad for her reputation, which made no sense. Like, how is some girl going missing bad for my sister's reputation?"

"You just don't understand how reputations work for girls," said Luke. "My sister Ashley has all kinds of rumors going around about her at school. You guys know exactly what I'm talking about." They did. Rumor had it that Luke's fifth-grade sister Ashley had been caught giving a classmate a hand job in the boys' bathroom right before spring break earlier in the year. No one could confirm it, but the fact that both she and Todd had been suspended at the same time was fairly telling that something, even if no one knew exactly what, had happened. "Still," Luke continued, "you can tell us. Besides, it's summer. Even if we wanted to be jerks and blab to the whole school about what happened, there's no one to tell."

"Not to mention," said Scott, "if Molly really is gone, everyone is going to know exactly what happened anyways. If she's really gone for more than a few days, it'll be on the news, like last summer, when that kid from Kentwood wound up dead in that refrigerator."

"I still don't get why anyone would hide in an old fridge," said Tim, trying to deflect the thought of Becca being anything like Luke's sisters. "You know it had to have smelled super bad in there. And you guys have a point. But you have to promise that you won't tell anyone. If the whole town finds out my sister was frenching some dude at the drive-in, that's fine, as long as they didn't find out from me, or from you. Got it?"

Scott and Luke did, both of their heads bobbling as Tim started to tell them what happened. "My sister wanted to go see a couple of movies at the drive-in, and—"

"What movies?"

"*The Untouchables* and *Full Met*—"

"Wait," said Scott. "Did she say if *Full Metal Jacket* was good? Carl and my mom saw it on Friday when it came out, and he said it was awesome. Seriously, you guys, my stepdad told me that movie would put hair on my balls. He said it was just like Nam, no Hollywood fucking around like *Apocalypse Now* or *Platoon*. I totally want to go, but Carl asked at the movie theater and they said no minors. I could tell it was good, 'cause my mom was freaking out, but—"

"Let Tim tell us what happened," said Luke. "Just give it a rest in general."

Scott sat down, looking pissed. Tim thought Luke was pretty harsh, calling him out like that—what about the blood-brothers business?—but went on with the story.

"So my sister and some friends went to the drive-in, most likely to drink beer and hit on older guys. The usual stuff."

"Stupid stuff," added Scott.

"Yes, exactly, super-stupid stuff. Anyways, something happened, I'm pretty sure between my sister and one of the guys.

Which is weird, because I know she is, like, in love with Tyler Cranston, but she says it wasn't him, and even sounded sort of PO'd that someone would even think it was. So my theory is this: My sister and her dumb buddies go to the drive-in. Something happens that makes Becca pissed at Tyler, probably saw him kissing another girl or something, and she decides to try and make him jealous. Only the older guy that she hooks up with wants to do more than just kiss."

"Like have sex or something?" Luke asked.

"Yeah, something like that. Maybe he was trying to go all the way. Who knows? Anyways, my sister made it clear she didn't want to do that, and something bad happened. When she came home her shirt was torn, and I could tell she was really upset. And not like how she gets upset when I call her Bacon and she's feeling fat, but really upset, and really scared too."

"Did any of the other girls hook up with some of the older guys too?" Scott asked. "'Cause maybe they did, and one of them took Molly. Maybe he's some psycho killer or something, like that guy dumping bodies in the park, and her saying no wouldn't have mattered at all."

"Yeah, right," said Luke. "A psychopath kidnapping some high school chick from a drive-in movie theater? That might happen downtown, but not here. You need to lose the late-night horror flicks, Scotty."

"I don't know, maybe Scott's on to something," said Tim. "After all, stuff like that always happens in places that seem pretty normal. That's how dudes like that get away with it for so long, because nobody wants to suspect their neighbor."

"Jesus," said Luke. "Both of you? You two need to soak your heads. Next thing you'll be telling me you think the Russkies are really going to nuke us, and we need to dig bomb shelters. If you guys want to go play private eye, you can be my guest. Just so you know, though, I'll be doing rad shit while you're gone, and when you come back, I'll be the one laughing. That girl is going to come home in a day or two with a broken heart and maybe a baby in her belly, and that's going to be the end of it. Trust me, give it a couple days, she'll come crawling back, and everyone except the high school kids will forget this ever happened."

Eager to change the subject, and feeling terrible for having shared the information in the first place, Tim said, "Anyways, the guns. You guys really want to give up on the target? I think it's fun to at least try."

"Tim," said Luke. "Let me level with you: Molly Peterson is a lot more likely to be really kidnapped than we are to hit that target with these shitty guns. I've got an hour left before I have to go home and make sure my idiot sisters remember to have lunch. You guys actually want to do anything, or just keep on yapping like old ladies?"

11

The three friends broke up the party fifteen minutes before Luke needed to be home to make lunch. If Luke was late, his sisters would tell on him. If he just skipped it, they wouldn't eat, and they'd tell on him. It was ridiculous, they were just a year younger than he was, but it was what his mom wanted, so he tolerated it with a skin that was growing thicker by the day.

Scott had invited Tim to come over to his house and eat—no one was home, Carl was working, and his mom had a week of doubles—but Tim declined. There was never anything exciting happening at home, and as bad as he felt for Becca, he did want to see if there were any new developments. Tim was smiling as he walked past the patio and into the front yard, but the sight of the unfamiliar car in the driveway changed that, mostly because the one behind it was a marked police car.

With a lump in his throat, along with a powerfully burning curiosity, Tim walked through his yard and bounded up the driveway to the front door. When he walked in, he stopped dead in his tracks.

Becca and his parents were sitting at the kitchen table with a man in a black suit, along with a uniformed police officer. Five sets of eyes turned to him as the door swung open, and Tim closed it behind him quietly. "Tim," said his mom. "Go to your room and read a book. No one is in trouble, and we'll explain in a little bit."

"OK, Mom," he said, before gliding as silently as he was able through the dining room, the kitchen, and the hallway that led to his room, as though it were possible to offend the police officers by being noisy. The one in the uniform had looked just like any cop Tim had ever seen: he was tall, with a broad chest, and had a really cool-looking pistol on his right hip. The detective, though, if that's what he was, had been different. Tim had been able to feel the man's eyes on him as soon as he'd entered the room, and he'd known he was being analyzed, judged. He was as sure of it as he was of anything, as if the detective had used some sort of impossible brain scan on him to see if there were any useful information trapped in his mind. *God, maybe Luke's right. Too many scary movies.* That wasn't how it felt, though. The detective had been sizing him up, chewing on Tim as if he were a fatty piece of steak, and it was not a comfortable feeling.

With the bedroom door closed behind him, Tim felt a lot better, as if that sort of barrier could possibly protect him from a detective with the ability to know exactly when and how a boy was lying. It was a weak barrier. Tim wanted to, in order: (1) tell those cops that he knew nothing, (2) play Nintendo in the family room—Zelda, always Zelda lately—and (3) go hang out with his friends. A soft knock on his door was a fair indicator that none of the above would be happening, and Tim exhaled softly as his dad entered the room following the light tap.

"How are you doing, big guy?" Stan asked, and Tim searched his father's face for information. There was nothing there. He looked like he always did, only maybe a little more tired than usual.

"I'm OK. What are those cops doing here?"

"They had to ask Becca some questions about last night." Stan sighed. "Letting her go to that movie keeps becoming a worse and worse decision, unfortunately. One of the girls that she went with,

Molly, didn't come home last night, and her mom is really upset, really worried. Not that I blame her for that. If Becca hadn't come home, your mom and I would be going nuts. I think any parent would. Anyways, Becca isn't in trouble or anything, at least not with the police. They just had to ask her when she last saw Molly, who she was with, things like that."

"What did she say?"

Stan took a deep breath. "She told them when she saw her last, and who she was with. Her description matched what some of the other girls had to say, and I think that made the cops happy that all their ducks were in a row."

"Is Molly going to be OK?"

"I don't know, buddy. I sure hope so, but I don't think the guys your sister and her friends were hanging around with were very nice people. Now, that doesn't mean that Molly won't turn out to be just fine—that's really the most likely thing. But it does make me worried for you guys, as a parent."

"You don't need to worry about me, Dad. I don't want to hang out with creepy older guys; plus, I never go to the drive-in, unless it's with you and Mom."

Stan let out a bark of laughter, and then looked down at Tim again. "That's good stuff. You get some lunch and go find something to do. It's summer. You don't want to be stuck up in your room all day. And remember, if you get bored, there's lots of hard work to be done out back."

—

Luke made it home with three minutes to spare. When he walked into the trailer, he saw his sisters sitting on the living room floor, watching a soap opera. From the sound of things, someone had been caught having an affair. Luke ignored them, and they ignored Luke as he passed them and went to the kitchen. As usual, his mom was nowhere to be found.

Luke took a jar of jelly from the refrigerator, and then a jar of peanut butter from the cupboard. He opened both jars, then placed three plates on the counter, topping them with bread that he quickly checked for mold. After spreading the sandwiches with peanut butter and jelly—lots of both for him; light jelly, heavy peanut butter for Alisha; light peanut butter, heavy jelly for Ashley—Luke topped the jellied pieces with the peanut butter–covered ones, then added chips to all three plates.

He carried his sisters' food into the living room and placed it before them, getting no reaction from the girls. Ignoring them in return, Luke walked back to the kitchen, poured himself a glass of Coke from a two-liter bottle, then sat at the lone clean spot at the dining room table. The table was covered with bills and laundry, and not for the first time, Luke wondered if his mom chose for them to live in filth, or if she just didn't know any other way. Deciding that was too depressing a thought to ponder, he began to imagine being screamed at by a drill instructor while he did push-ups. In the fantasy it was raining, he was knuckle deep in mud, and he was smiling. *Someday.*

When Luke was done eating, he put his plate in the sink and walked to the living room. His sisters were where he had left them—one on the floor, one lying across the couch—and both of their plates were empty. The soap opera was still blaring from the TV as Luke passed in front of their glassy-eyed faces to collect the dishes, and once they were retrieved, he headed back to the kitchen. Luke set the plates in the sink with his, then turned on the water and laid a towel down upon the counter so that he would have space to let them dry. *Mom doesn't work but is almost never home. Where does she go?* This thought, much like the one concerning the condition of their house, was almost too black to really put much energy into. Luke felt quite certain that no matter what his mom filled her days with, it was probably better not to know.

When the dishes were done, Luke noticed a familiar smell coming from the other room. Drying his hands with the same towel he used as a drying rag, Luke walked into the living room, where he saw his sisters smoking cigarettes, flicking the ashes into their mom's pilfered Arby's ashtrays.

"You guys can't smoke in the house!" Luke bellowed. "If Mom finds out you guys were stealing her cigarettes, she'll kill you, not to mention what she'll do if she catches you smoking in the house."

"But she won't catch us," said Ashley, blowing a ring of far-too-practiced smoke from her lips. "Because we didn't steal Mom's cigarettes," finished Alisha. "We told her that we smoked a few weeks ago, and she's been buying them for us ever since."

"But that doesn't make any sense," stammered Luke. "We're broke. Why would Mom let you do that? Not to mention it's terrible for you. Everybody knows that."

"We're not smoking a lot," said Alisha. "That's why you haven't seen us smoking before." She exhaled another blast of nicotine and tar. "Besides, Mom told us it would help us keep our figures," said Ashley. "I'm not going to get all fat and gross. Plus, guys like girls who smoke. Mom told us that too."

"I'm leaving," said Luke quietly. "I'll be back for dinner."

"Fine," said Ashley, her eyes already focused on the TV, her lipstick-stained cigarette dangling from her fingers. "Yeah," seconded Alisha. "Of course you are. You're never home unless it's time to eat. You might be older than us, but you sure act like a kid. All you do is run around in the woods with your stupid friends. You're totally wasting your summer."

"All you two do is watch TV," said Luke. "And apparently now you smell bad doing it."

"Luke," said Ashley. "You have no idea what we do when you're not around." She stubbed her cigarette in a foil ashtray and returned her focus to the television. "Yeah," said Alisha, punching out her own butt. "We have big plans, and you don't have a clue."

Luke turned from them, let the door slam shut, and began to walk to the fort. When he got there he dropped his Sprite cap on the ground and began to climb the ladder. Just like the cap on the ground, he was alone in the woods.

———

Scott walked to the mailbox, one last thing to do before he could rejoin his friends. Lunch had been boring as usual, no one was home to talk to, and there was nothing good to watch on TV during the day. *This summer sucks so far.* The target was supposed to give them days of fun, but all it really did was show them that make-believe went only so far.

He watched as a police cruiser rolled slowly down the street toward him, followed closely by a matching car that was missing police markings. The cruiser slipped past him, but the other car eased to a stop across the street, even with him. The cruiser stopped too. Scott gave a look behind him, but there was no one there. The driver's window of the car without the markings rolled down, and a younger-looking guy hung out an arm holding a wallet and a piece of paper.

"Come over here, son," called the man in the car. "I need to ask you a couple of questions."

Wary of the stranger, but comforted by the presence of the definitely-a-police-car idling in front of him, Scott slowly walked into the street to the car. "What can I help you with?"

The man in the car flipped open the wallet, and inside it was a picture of him, along with a silver badge. "I'm a detective with the Grand Rapids Police Department," he said. "And right now, we're looking for a missing girl. Seen anything odd out in the woods back there today?"

"No," said Scott. "How did you know I was in the woods?"

The detective pointed at his shoes. They were dirty, and did sort of look like he'd been in the woods. "Oh, OK," said Scott. "But no, I haven't seen anything weird. I'm going back there to meet some friends, though. We can keep a lookout."

"What grade are you in, son?" asked the detective, who made the wallet disappear and then handed Scott a black-and-white photocopy of a picture of Molly Peterson. It looked like a school photo.

"I'm going into seventh," said Scott.

"You're tall for your age," said the detective. "I would have figured freshman, maybe sophomore by your build. You were not at the drive-in last night, then?"

"No," said Scott, shaking his head. "Is Molly really missing?"

"She is," said the detective, who pulled the photo back into the car. The hand came back with a card, which the detective pressed into Scott's hand. It said, "Detective Richard Van Endel" and had a phone number. "If you or your buddies come across anything in those woods, call this number. It's my direct line."

"Do you think she's back there?"

"I think she's somewhere, and there's an old trail that leads from behind the screen of that movie theater." Van Endel shrugged. "Just keep your eyes open."

"I will," said Scott, as the window rolled up and the car started to move. He looked at the card in his cupped palm. *Cool.*

12

Detective Van Endel sat in Dr. Andrea Martinez's office. Martinez was a leggy Hispanic woman with ample breasts and a beautiful caramel skin tone. She was also a lesbian, not currently dating, and took judo twice a week. Those who thought she was just an arm piece waiting for the right arm were sadly mistaken, and discovered as much quickly. Dr. Martinez had been working with the Grand Rapids Police Department off and on for the past few years, and Van Endel valued her counsel more than just about anyone else's. This was not the first case he had asked for her thoughts on, and it was not going to be the last.

"So give me your first impression," said Dr. Martinez. "Is she gone?"

"She's gone," said Van Endel. "But there's more to it than that. The kids I talked to are all telling the same story, but it feels rehearsed. Not to mention, I know the shit kids get into at that drive-in. Nothing like this has ever made anyone turn tail, from what I've heard. I mean, a little making out goes a little too far, girl's friends help her get away from the guy, end of story."

"I wouldn't treat attempted rape quite so flippantly, Dick," said Dr. Martinez. "The number of unreported rapes in this country—in this *county*—is growing astronomically. There is no use debating that." She smiled. "Especially with me."

"I'm not treating anything flippantly," said Van Endel. "My point is that there's probably something illegal happening at that drive-in almost every day involving teenagers, and I just don't see this big of a group of them freaking out over one girl getting groped and then leaving without a friend. I know they said they went back for her, but I don't think they did. I just don't think we're getting even half the real story."

"What do the drive-in employees say?"

"I talked to the crew from last night. Pretty much worst-case scenario there. Gus Lembowski was sick, and he had a couple deadbeats running the projector and the food. I'm sure they barely accomplished either one. By the time I got there, the marijuana smoke had cleared out and they were out picking up garbage from last night."

"Details?"

"They saw a bunch of teens come in like they do every night that they work. I asked if a large group left early, they said that they did. I asked if they could identify any of the vehicles or people in them, they said they couldn't, not even the make of one single car. I asked if there were any fights, or other disturbances that stuck out to them, they said no." He rolled his eyes. "Godzilla would have to have shown up to watch a movie for those two to take notice of it."

"So there's no proof the kids were there or not, right?"

"None. Which means I have to follow the drive-in as a lead, even though my gut tells me it's a load of crap."

"What does your gut say?" Dr. Martinez asked. "To go sit at Riverside and wait for him to drop her off? Not to be a bother, but aside from there being a possible female victim, this doesn't fit with our ideas about that guy, nor does it fit the MO of those crimes. You may just have to accept that you're not going to get the whole story from the kids. Kids' first response is to clam up when they're lying, and they do the same thing when they're nervous."

Van Endel stood, walked to the coffee carafe on a table near the window, and poured himself a cup. He took it black, so the absence of cream wasn't a problem. He nodded to the coffee, and she shook her head.

"They're lying, not nervous," said Van Endel, still standing. "I absolutely believe there were some beers and maybe even some grass tied in with what they were up to. That could even be the reason their story smells like rotten fish. God, if she really just did run off and I'm getting the runaround because a few suburban princes and princesses don't want Mommy and Daddy to find out they kifed a few beers from somebody's garage…" He shook his head. "No. You know, the hell with that. I wouldn't even be upset. Just let the girl go home, and I'm good. They can have the secrets."

"But what if they're lying for another reason?"

"Well, that, Doc, is what I keep coming back to. Like you said, my gut says to go wait in the park with a bunch of unis and see what happens." He sat again, heavily, then set the coffee on a coaster that she placed in front of him. "Here's where I'm at. The kids are lying about something, I know it. What I don't know is why they're lying, or if it actually matters to the case or not. I also know that the guys who work at that fucking drive-in are idiots, and that they could have seen everything, and it wouldn't matter. What's your take?"

"I think your girl was taken by someone at the drive-in," said Dr. Martinez. "The kids all insisted that's where they were, from what you've told me, and until it's proven otherwise, that's what you need to work with, isn't it? Seems you'd have to stick with the drive-in angle and hope for the best. Unfortunately, it's about all you've got, isn't it?"

"That's about what I figured you'd say. Until someone comes forward, she walks home, or, God forbid, we find her somewhere, I'm up the river, sans paddle." Van Endel finished the coffee and dropped the Styrofoam cup into the trash. "One more thing, Doc. I need help. Phil's on leave…"

"Say no more," said Martinez, smiling. "I'll do my best to clear my schedule, and, God willing, we'll find your girl."

13

Hooper had Amy tied to a chair in the living room, the late-morning sun falling in bands across her through the drawn blinds. She was sitting still and shaking slightly, but was otherwise unable to move. In her mouth was a gag—rags and a belt, which had proven quite effective. She was bound to the chair with a mixture of nautical rope and ratcheting straps, the straps around her chest binding her tightly to the chair. Looking at her, he couldn't help but smile. He had his colt, now he just needed to break her.

Hooper still smelled like smoke from the fire behind the back fence of the closed drive-in late the night before. It was in his clothes and in his hair, dirt still under his fingernails from digging. He needed a shower desperately, not to mention some sleep, but he was scared to let her out of his sight for even a moment, lest Amy try and leave again, like she'd done when he went to Southeast Asia. Having her here was as much a burden as it was a pleasure, but the risks of the situation needed to be respected. *There has to be a better way to bind her up that won't allow her to escape or hurt herself, but will also allow me to touch her.*

The thought of fucking her was not a new one for Hooper. He had been with his sister several times before he left for the war, getting to her before she was spoiled goods, the leavings of another man. The same might not be true with this Amy, but he needed to find out for himself, so that he could pleasure them both. It was going to be wonderful. He just needed to be sure of how to keep her captive before he broke down to his baser desires and took her.

Finally deciding that she wasn't going anywhere, Hooper began to strip off his clothing in front of her. Amy's eyes were shut tightly, but he didn't care. She was going to see him eventually one way or the other.

Hooper walked to the shower and turned the water on as hot as it would go. He stepped into the still-cold stream and felt his muscles twitch reflexively. *There is such peace in the shower.* In the shower Hooper could be himself. He wasn't some broken-down Vietnam vet between jobs. Under the water, he felt impossibly alive and full of hope. The finally hot water gave him clarity as it all but scalded his skin, and he realized that what he needed most, more even than a better restraint system, was a plan.

When Hooper had taken women against their will before, it had been a temporary thing, short-term. He had initially been thinking of the same fate for Amy, but in a twist of whimsy, he'd decided to keep her for a while. That posed other risks. Carl, another vet and friend, had mentioned a week or so ago that he needed help working on his wife's car, and Hooper had agreed to help. But how could he leave Amy alone in the house? There were a million things that could go wrong.

Hooper hadn't been watching the news, but if the girl really had just been playing at prostitution, it was likely that people everywhere were looking for her. There was hardly any media coverage when the other bodies were found, but a regular girl was sure to garner much more public interest than a prostitute. Though he loathed doing so, Hooper was going to have to keep up with the news. With the other whores, there had been no connection to him, nothing left on the body for some supercop to link back to him. With Amy in the house, though, there was plenty of evidence that could be used to destroy his life, and Hooper was not going to let that happen.

So, to keep myself safe, I need for Amy to be safe. Safe would mean no possibility of escape, a perfect place and way for her to be kept and yet still be accessible to him. The basement seemed to make the most sense, but there were two windows down there, and if she escaped her restraints at night, she could possibly make her way out of the house until it was far too late for him to do something about it. If only he had planned, had considered even for a moment that he might someday want to keep one of them. It was no wonder that he hadn't, though. They were so expendable, like the girl he'd killed the night before.

Hooper had taken her just to cover his tracks, in case Amy was telling the truth and her friends gave up to the police what they'd been up to and where she'd really been. If they did, someone was going to have seen his car, maybe even remember the license plate number if he was really unlucky. The burned body by the drive-in could change all that, slow down the investigation as the sands of truth fell to the bottom bell of the hourglass. If the friends she claimed to have been with kept up the lie for even a few days, the discovery of the body would make it unnecessary for them to tell the truth—as far as they knew, their friend would be dead, so why get themselves in trouble? Hooper still wasn't sure exactly what game had been afoot, he just knew that it had allowed him to take Amy, and for that he was grateful.

The shower ran cold, and Hooper bent to turn it off. They never seemed to last long enough, and he could feel the clarity from the solitude of the running water falling swiftly away. He dried himself quickly and hung the towel on a hook next to the shower. He considered going to the bedroom to get clothes, but instead walked back to Amy. *I can shop for what I need tomorrow. Now I want to be with her.* Her eyes widened as he entered the room, and he could see her struggling with the chair. He smiled to himself as he circled behind her bound form.

"You need to learn to calm down," said Hooper. Not for the first time, he wished he'd learned something of medicine in Southeast Asia, but he hadn't. NyQuil might do the trick. If it didn't, booze would. "I can get something to help you relax," said Hooper. "But for right now, how about something to eat?" He ran his fingers through her hair, and she jerked away from him. "You've got to be hungry," he said, cupping her chin and looking into her eyes. She was tearing up, no longer feeling tough. For Hooper, seeing her already beginning to crack was like receiving a gift from God. "Good girl. I'll make you some toast, and if you can eat it and don't try and scream, maybe we'll talk about what I need from you." She nodded her head slowly, tears streaking her cheeks. *Perfect.*

14

"I still don't think it means anything," said Luke. "So some detective is driving around and asking questions, so what? That's just his job. I say she turns up in a day or so, tired and maybe still a little hungover."

"It's not like all we want to do is go rummaging around the woods," said Tim. "But we would be, like, the coolest if she were lost back there, or hurt or something, and we found her."

"Or dead," said Luke. "Or say we do play cops, like you guys want, and we find her with her guts torn out? Have either of you thought about that? You know, considered the actual bad parts of this, and not just thought, *Oh, cool, cops are at my house*? Where I live, the cops' being at your house is really uncool. The reality is that if she is out there, she's probably dead, and I'm not going to lie, I don't need to see that."

"What crawled up your ass?" Scott asked. "So what if we think it's cool that we got to talk to the cops or whatever? It *is* pretty cool."

"Whatever."

"Look," said Tim, trying to bring reasonableness back to a normally very reasonable Luke. "We don't need to do anything. If we decide we want to go look for clues or whatever, we'll do it as a group. Just like everything else that we do, and you know that," he said, pointing at Luke. "But what is it with you lately?"

"What do you mean?" Luke asked, but he kept his eyes on the floor.

"I don't *know* what I mean, but you're, like, all…I don't know, lately. *Something's* going on with you. It's obvious. If you want to tell us what's really going on, I wish you'd just go for it."

"It's everything, OK?" Luke said hoarsely, his friends thinking that he might actually cry, and how scary that might be. Crying was for skinned knees, not emotional breakdowns. "Everything in my life is getting so fucked up. You want to know something crazy? I made my sisters' lunch like an hour ago, and you know what they were doing? Smoking. They're eleven years old and they smoke cigarettes, and apparently my mom is totally fine with it. They don't have to do anything but sit around and watch TV, and I have to do everything. Plus, my mom doesn't work, and she's never home. Even when she's there, she's on the phone all the time, just totally forgetting the fact that she has these three kids she's supposed to take care of. Plus, she's fucked up all the time. And not like when one of you guys' dads has too many beers or whatever. I mean she gets really fucked up, like, pisses her pants or throws up on herself."

There was a long moment when none of them talked or looked at each other. The sounds of the forest trickled into the fort, and then a lawn mower started up somewhere.

Finally Scott said, "That sucks, man. Seriously. But if it helps at all, no one has a perfect life. At least you see your dad a few times a year. I never see mine. And don't tell me how that doesn't count because Carl's cool. Carl isn't my dad, and he never will be—he's just Carl. So yeah, if I went through all the rotten stuff in my life, I bet I could feel pretty bad for myself too, but I don't. Not everybody has it easy like Tim."

"Hey!"

"I'm just messing with you," said Scott, punching Tim lightly on the arm, and then turning back to Luke. "You need to look at things like that counselor lady told us: 'Your glass needs to be half full.'"

"That's fine," said Luke. "But what do I do if I don't have a glass?"

"She didn't say anything about that."

"I figured as much," said Luke. "They never tell us the stuff we really need to know."

———

After a day basically wasted sitting in the fort, Scott was almost excited to go home for dinner. On the way there, he kept his eyes peeled for some sort of disturbance, something glaringly different, but, of course, he saw nothing. That sort of thing seemed to be reserved for the movies, like digging for dinosaur bones and actually finding them.

The air was cool as he walked through the woods, and he could smell at least one person barbecuing, the smell of suburban summers that never got old.

Luke was a wreck, there was no debating it, and Scott had no idea what to do for his friend. He wanted to talk to Tim about it, but the three of them were always together, and there was no good time for it. *I could call him later*, but that would mean he wouldn't have any privacy. If his mom heard even half of what was happening at Luke's house, she'd call the cops in a second.

Scott had a hard time believing it at first. Why would an adult be so shitty at being an adult? It just didn't make any sense. His dad's leaving made no sense, and now Luke's mom, Emma, made no sense. It almost made him question adulthood in general. *What if they're all just faking it? What if none of them has the slightest idea what they're doing?*

The sight of smoke billowing up from behind his house made Scott whoop with joy. Whatever else had gone wrong with the day, Carl was grilling, and even the worst of days can still finish well with a good dinner.

Carl was standing in front of the grill, drinking a can of Miller Lite, and Carl never drank during the week. For a very brief moment, Scott was terrified. Maybe everything was falling apart here too, and the goings-on at Luke's house could be explained away easily: "The adults all went crazy." Carl's smile made everything OK, though, and, passing through the kitchen of the house, Scott opened the screen door and went back outside.

"Scott, my man," said Carl, finishing the beer and grabbing a fresh one from the cooler at his feet. "How's it hanging?"

Not sure how to respond, Scott finally settled on "I'm doing good. What are you making?"

"Steak," said Carl, between swigs of beer. "You and I are celebrating. I got some New Yorks from the butcher, and he says they are going to melt in our mouths. I took him at his word and bought the biggest two that he had. Sounds good, right?"

"Yeah," said Scott. "It sounds awesome. But what are we celebrating?" Carl finished the second beer in epic time, then cracked a third and took a deep swig. "Well," said Carl, "between the two of us, I just got promoted at work. Which is pretty cool. Not quite beer-on-a-Tuesday cool or, hell, steak-on-a-night-that-your-mom-works cool, but still pretty cool.

"And there's an even cooler part. This wasn't just a little old raise, this was the spot I've been gunning for, and you know what? No more waiting tables for my wife, guaranteed. No more truck leaking oil, either, at least once we get used to the larger checks. I am officially going to be managing a team of guys, instead of just running a machine. Nice, eh?"

"Mom will really be able to stop working?"

"Yep. I even considered stopping by her work and making her quit tonight, but I know Beth would have said no, and would have insisted on putting in her two weeks so she doesn't screw anybody over. This is pretty good news for us, Scott. For all three of us."

"It's amazing."

"Yep, but there's something else amazing that I need too. Go run down to the basement and fetch up one of my jars of steak sauce. These are good cuts, so no A.1. tonight. We'll use my morel sauce."

"Sweet," said Scott. He'd had the morel sauce twice, and it *was* amazing. His stepdad went mushrooming for weeks in the spring, searching under fallen elms for the delicious and difficult-to-find wild fungus. Carl made the sauce once a year, and Scott was pretty sure his stepdad could bottle it for sale if he were able to find enough mushrooms to make it happen. That, of course, was never going to happen: morels commanded a hefty price at market, and the unpredictability of finding the things meant even the family supply was quite finite.

The only thing more surprising than sharing steaks and the sauce with his stepfather, though, was access to the basement. "Do I need a key or something?" For as long as Scott could remember, the basement was do not enter, all Carl's.

"Nope," said Carl. "Truth told, Scott, I haven't locked it in years. I trust you, buddy. Maybe you trust me a bit too. Maybe this new job, and your mom quitting hers, will make you trust me even more. We're a family, kid, a modern family. We don't need blood to be one." Carl paused, then said, "So go get a bottle of sauce, give the armory a look, no touching, and bring it back up."

"Yes, sir," said Scott, and he meant it.

———

The basement was cold. The summer was not hot in June of 1987, but being in a cooler environment was still very inviting. Scott figured it was below seventy degrees downstairs, maybe even cooler. Even better than just being cooler was that he'd never been down there without Carl, except to do laundry, and that was in a totally different room. At the bottom of the stairs, Scott walked past the washer and dryer to the door he had assumed was always locked, then turned the knob and walked inside.

On one wall was a long table, atop which was a table clamp, along with the tools necessary for the manufacture of ammunition. Also on the table were a few boxes of rifle ammunition that had been assembled, along with a few tins of powder and boxes of unloaded cartridges. Next to the table was a drop-front desk that was closed, and—Scott was sure without even checking—locked. Above the desk were three sets of whitetail deer antlers, all mounted in the European style, with just plates of skull and horns on display.

On the wall across from the desk and table were three gun racks, all of them festooned with various rifles and shotguns, including one rifle with an odd-looking stock that Scott had seen once before. It was an AR-7, manufactured by Charter Arms and chambered in .22 Long Rifle. The entire gun could be broken down and stored within the stock, and was easily assembled with no tools. Eugene Stoner, the man who had invented the M-16, had come up with the AR-7 earlier in his career as a compact weapon to be used by pilots who were shot down. Carl had purchased it to use as a sort of trail gun to shoot small game, or for highly unlikely self-defense scenarios, on a trip that had yet to be taken. *It would be perfect for shooting at the target. The fort would eat up most of the noise, and the bullets wouldn't travel far enough to hurt someone by accident.* Scott ran his fingers over the black composite stock, then drew them away, as if it were hot.

Ashamed at his speedy betrayal of his stepdad's trust, Scott walked to a rack at the back of the room covered in canned fruit, along with jars of homemade steak and barbecue sauce. He grabbed a bottle of the steak sauce, then walked back to the door, giving the racks of guns one final look before heading back upstairs. The AR-7 was dancing in his mind, and the conversation with the detective, along with the business card in his pocket, all but forgotten.

15

Hooper whistled as he walked through the hardware section at Meijer Wednesday morning. He was back, buying supplies to make a pair of different restraints, and was wearing sunglasses and a Detroit Tigers cap, just in case. His cart already held chains, heavy-gauge rope, ratcheting straps, a pair of locks, and a few short two-by-fours. He had also gone shopping on Division Avenue, near the stretch where he had happened upon Amy in the first place. There he bought a pair of leg cuffs, a pair of handcuffs, a metal collar that locked and had a steel ring hanging from it, a rubber ball gag, and an enormous purple silicone cock. The sales clerk had made no mention of what Hooper was buying, just took his cash and said, "Have fun." Hooper couldn't help smiling as he left the store. What a world, where a man could buy such things in a store.

After perusing all of the wonderful things the hardware section had to offer, Hooper walked his nearly full cart to the opposite side of the store. There he threw a couple bottles of mascara, some nail polish, and tubes of lipstick into his cart. He wasn't exactly sure what he was looking for, but figured he'd just have to start somewhere, keep experimenting with different colors or brands until he had her looking just right. It was going to be a learning process, and he couldn't wait for it to begin.

Hooper also bought some groceries. He was used to subsisting mostly on rice and dehydrated foods, all stuff he'd grown accustomed to in the military, but he decided Amy's palate was probably different from his. At least until she could tell him what she liked to eat, he bought a few cans of soup, another loaf of bread, and a bottle of orange juice. He also threw a large bottle of NyQuil into the cart, along with a fifth of 190-proof Everclear. Ready to leave, he checked out at the front of the store, paying cash for his odd assortment of goods.

Once everything was loaded into the car, he fired up the engine on the old Dodge and turned on the radio. Bon Jovi was playing "Livin' on a Prayer," and Hooper drummed his thumbs on the steering wheel along with the music. He couldn't wait to get home, show her all the things he'd bought for her, and then put the ball in her mouth and lead her to the basement in chains. He didn't want to keep her there, but she was the furthest thing from housebroken, and it would be easiest to keep her chained up down there with the gag in her mouth, especially while he built the rack. He could picture her fastened to it in his mind, and the mental images were wonderful. She was his little bird, and he couldn't wait to admire her plumage.

As he drove down suburban streets, he couldn't help but feel a little proud of himself. How many of the men who occupied these homes could say that they had accomplished what he had in life? He was a man's man, a veteran injured in war, a man who took what he wanted, the rules of society be damned. Sure, he didn't have much money, or a job, but he had what few else did: a real sense of freedom, freedom he had earned in a trial by fire. The world might not have planned much for Matt Hooper, but that didn't mean he couldn't tear off a big old hunk of living when God wasn't looking.

He parked in the driveway, beaming, the plain brown paper bag from the fuck store in one hand, a bag of food from Meijer in the other. He opened the door awkwardly and slipped through it, looking to his left for Amy. She was gone.

Hooper dropped the bag and slammed the door behind him. *Oh fuck oh fuck oh fuck*, the thoughts a cadence, his headache immediate.

He ran to the kitchen and found her struggling with the sliding door, dressed in a pair of his shorts and a T-shirt. He crossed the house to her, moving fast as hell, but she slipped through the slider, already starting to scream. He grabbed a black and very loaded Colt 1911 from the drawer by the door, thanked God silently that she hadn't looked there, and then was out the door after her. She was working open the gate in his wood fence, and then was through it and into the woods. If she had looked or run right or left, he would have been fucked, but she didn't, she went straight into the trees, and he ran after her.

16

Tim woke a few hours after the sun came up that morning and, after brushing his teeth, taking a quick shower, and dressing, headed to the kitchen. He could see his dad out back working, but also saw storm clouds overhead. *Dad will be so happy if it rains for a little while,* Tim thought, a grin passing over his face. He dropped two pieces of white bread into the toaster, then grabbed a butter knife and a plate. He could hear his mom and Becca talking down the hallway, but couldn't hear and didn't care what they were saying. His toast popped, he buttered it, and he sat down at the table.

The *Grand Rapids Press* from the day before lay open on the table. As he flipped past the first few sections to find the sports and comics, a picture of Molly stopped Tim cold. *She's still missing.* Seeing her there in print made it real somehow. She was missing, and maybe she really wasn't coming back.

The picture also gave Tim pause. If no one was searching the woods yet, maybe that task did fall to him and his friends. After all, they knew the area better than anyone. Adults rarely went back there, and most teenagers preferred to party in Provin Trails, or at the drive-in. Tim finished his toast, forgetting all about the funnies, the sports section, and finding the fifth dungeon in Zelda. He wanted to go to the fort.

After dropping his plate in the sink, Tim walked outside. His dad was transferring rocks from the wheelbarrow. "You see that, buddy?" Stan asked. "Those look like storm clouds. Can you say 'day off'?"

Tim shielded his eyes with his right hand. "I don't know, Dad. Those just look like regular clouds."

Stan sighed and threw another shovel full of pea gravel into the hole. "You could throw a guy a bone once in a while."

"You know, Dad," said Tim, "now that you mention it, maybe those are storm clouds. I'm going to the woods. Do you think I should bring an umbrella?"

Stan grinned back at him as he worked the shovel. "That's more like it. Are you going to be back for lunch?"

"I think so," said Tim. "If I go to Scott's, I'll call."

"Sounds good," said Stan. "How are those guys doing? I haven't seen Scott or Luke since the deck teardown."

"They're good," said Tim, wondering whether or not he should tell his dad about Luke. It wouldn't be like telling his mom. If he told his dad, it probably would stay between them, unless things were worse with Luke than he thought. That was the problem, though. Luke had a flair for drama, he always had, and maybe this was just more of that. Or, worse, maybe he was sugarcoating an even worse situation so that he could still vent about it a little without having one of them get help. There wasn't any right thing for Tim to do, that he could see.

"Tim?"

"Yeah?"

"You looked like you kind of shut down for a second there. I know it's been a little crazy around here lately. Is there anything you want to tell me?"

"No," said Tim, really wondering if he was making the right choice now. "Everything is fine."

He was wrong.

———

When Tim got to the fort there were two bottle caps lying at the base of the ladder, Sprite and Coke. He threw down his own Budweiser cap, then began to climb up. When he got to the top, he saw Scott and Luke sitting together and staring at something Scott was holding. "Took you long enough," said Scott. "We've been waiting for what felt like forever."

Closer to them now, Tim could see what Scott was holding: a new air rifle, or was it—

"It's the real thing, Tim," said Luke. "A real rifle." He held up a cartridge. It had a small copper bullet, along with a smooth brass casing. "Here's yours," Luke continued, before handing Tim the bullet. "We all get to shoot it once, and we're going to have a rock-paper-scissors tournament to see who shoots first."

"Are you sure that's a good idea?" Tim asked. "If we get caught shooting back here, that's going to be the end of summer."

"You're telling me," said Scott. "That's Carl's gun. If he knew I took it, much less fired it, I think he might just decide it would be easier to kill me than to come up with a big enough punishment."

"So why did you take it?"

"Because we all want to shoot at that target. And besides, we're not going to be hurting anybody. We're going to shoot the gun three times, break it back down, and then walk to my house to put it away. We don't even have to clean it, because it's still dirty from when Carl sighted it in."

"I'm not sure this is a good idea."

"We're going to shoot it either way," said Luke, who from the sound of his voice had forgotten the problems of the day prior. "Whether you want to or not. We're not going to get caught, either. Almost all of the noise will be absorbed by the fort, and that thing's not going to be much louder than our air rifles. I already beat Scott at rock-paper-scissors, so you have to go against me to see who gets the first shot, and then the loser will go against Scott to see who shoots second. Are you in, or are you out?"

"In," said Tim with a grin, and Luke and Tim squared off in the center of the fort, while Scott, cradling the rifle, said, "Best two out of three." Luke had his right fist set down on his upturned palm, and Tim did the same, still grinning. "One, two, three," the boys said together, and Luke stayed with rock, while Tim opted for scissors.

They repeated the action again, this time with Tim pulling rock and Luke going scissors. The final outcome was determined when Tim defeated Luke with paper over rock. "We should have flipped coins or something," said Luke, a dark look on his face.

"No sour grapes," said Scott, laughing. "You agreed that this was the fairest way to decide who went first. You ready to see who goes second?"

"Yeah," said Luke, the dark look already fading. "I beat you once, Scotty, I can beat you again."

"All right, then, here we go," said Scott. "Best two out of three."

17

Amy was into the woods like a wild and finally loosed animal. Hooper was fit, but still had trouble keeping up with her, losing her visually only to find her a nerve-shattering second later, over and over again. Branches tugged at his skin, and brambles and thorns stuck in his shirt and hair, but he noticed none of the pain, ignoring everything except her.

She ran with an awkward gait, scrambling this way and that in a blind panic, tearing through trees seemingly at random, but heading toward the drive-in movie theater. If she made it there before him, there would be space for her to move in almost any direction, and if there was someone working, maintenance most likely, he would be forced to kill that person, and maybe even kill her too.

The cap and glasses were barely staying on his head, and Hooper kept having to fix them with his hands. If ever there was a time when he wished he were wearing a disguise, this was it, but the ball cap and sunglasses would have to do. The pistol was growing heavy in his hand. He'd never have chosen it as a carry piece, but in the time of need it had been his only option. *When I catch her and get her back to the house, I'm going to beat the shit out of her, and I'm going to fuck her every which way but loose.* The thought of punishing her lent speed to his legs, and for the first time since the chase had begun, Hooper began gaining ground on her.

She slowed as she crossed a small creek—sharp rocks don't go well with bare feet, figured Hooper. He almost had her then, but she must have sensed it, picking up the pace as his fingers nearly touched her back. She darted away from his touch as though he had poison running through his veins. It was painful to see Amy running away from him all over again.

Finally, she leapt over a downed tree, and must have twisted her ankle or caused some other injury to herself, because she screamed and went down. Hooper winced at the sound and then hopped over the log, letting the Colt lead the way. Her eyes went a mile wide at the sight of it, and she backed up tight against the log.

"You need to shut the fuck up right now," said Hooper. "Unless you want to get shot, get your ass up." The gag had fallen out of her mouth at some point during the chase, and she was heaving air into and out of her lungs so quickly that Hooper was scared she might hyperventilate. "C'mon, it ain't all that bad. Get up and relax a little bit. You're going to pass out if you don't."

She screamed again then, and Hooper slapped her with the hand not holding the pistol. The noise stopped immediately, and he held up his hand like he might do it again if she gave him reason enough to. "You good?" She nodded, and Hooper knew he had her.

Amy led the way, Hooper walking behind her with the pistol buried in her back. She was no longer crying, and seemed to Hooper almost resigned to what was happening. Her dark hair hung in matted strands, and, not for the first time, Hooper ached to wash her. She wasn't street trash like the rest of them. He wanted Amy clean, he needed her sparkling, done up and polished, but not as slutty as when he'd picked her up. All those things were going to happen once they got out of the goddamn woods, Hooper promised himself. It was time to break her, to make her give herself to him. He'd gotten lucky in catching her, but she'd gotten luckier by momentarily escaping. He couldn't wait to get home and figure out how she'd done it, and he knew that with the stuff he'd bought today, it wasn't going to be happening again.

18

Luke had beaten Scott after falling behind one–nothing and then scoring twice with paper to get the victory. Scott soured momentarily, but Luke perked up after the win.

Tim had been given the rifle, a single bullet, and a magazine to put the bullet into. Though the gun was semiauto, the boys hadn't even had to discuss firing it in such a way, as that would almost undoubtedly bring angry parents, or worse, down on them.

Tim slid the little bullet into the magazine and then pushed the magazine into the AR-7's tiny mag well, where it clicked into place with the satisfying sound of oiled metal on metal. "I pull this back to rack it, right?" Tim asked, and Scott nodded. Tim did so and was surprised at the effort it took. Then, once it was as far back as it could be pulled, he let go of the charging handle. It snapped back into place, and the gun was ready. "I'm kind of nervous," said Tim. "Now that we're really doing it. What if it's, like, super loud?"

"It won't be," said Luke. "You saw how little the bullet was. It's going to be loud to us, but only because we're stuck in here. Somebody outside will just think it's a firecracker." Thunder rumbled in the distance. "Even better, they'll think it's just more thunder."

Dad was right, Tim thought as he laid the barrel of the .22 on the windowsill. *I guess it is going to storm.*

He slowly shrugged his body around the gun, with his chin laid on the stock, just like they did with their air rifles. His finger was still off the trigger when it thundered again, louder this time, making him jump. Tim rested the barrel of the gun on the bottom of the windowsill and watched the front sight stop shaking in front of him. He took a deep breath, let it out slowly, and then began to acquire the target.

Luke was on his right side, Scott on his left, and the other boys were watching the target, wishing it was their turn, and waiting for the crack of the rifle.

The blade of the front sight was hovering between the ears of the rear sight, floating up and down with Tim's heartbeat, settling over the target, then leaving, then coming back to the center of the target. Not making a good shot when he got only one try would be a colossal failure, and Tim took in a breath, let half of it out, and slowly began to pull back on the trigger. It was creaking under his finger, moving ever so slowly backward, when Luke whispered, "Holy shit. Look."

"I'm trying to aim," said Tim. "We're all going to get a turn, so you don't need to be a dick about it."

"Seriously," whispered Luke. "Look in the pines over there. Tell me I'm not crazy." Scott and Tim both did, though Tim left the gun pointed more or less at the target, and blindly made it safe with his fingers. They both saw it at the same time, and as the man and the woman emerged from the pines, less than thirty yards from where they were sitting, they knew that Luke wasn't crazy.

The woman was crying, had black curly hair, and was being pushed ahead by the man. He had something in her back, though none of them could tell what, and when it thundered again they all jumped. It was obvious to all three of the boys that the girl was Molly Peterson, or someone who looked a great deal like her, but the man's features were indistinguishable. Rain began to fall in the forest, and they could see two things: Molly and the man were heading back to somewhere in the suburban neighborhood where Scott and Tim lived, and the man was pressing a gun into her back.

"You have to shoot him, Tim," said Luke. "Like, right now." Tim felt as though he'd been punched in the face. You were never supposed to point a gun at someone else, but on the other hand, the man was pointing a gun at Molly. "This might be her only chance," hissed Luke, louder now, as the rain began to fall more forcefully. "If you can't do it, give me the goddamn gun."

The next moments would last forever in Tim's mind, as the world slowed around him. He shouldered the rifle, put the front sight over the center of the man's back, and flicked the safety off. His finger began to tense on the trigger, and he let out a deep breath, then moved away from the window and fumbled the gun to Luke and Scott. Scott was pale, backing away from the rifle as if it were on fire, and Luke took the weapon. "I can't do it," said Tim, with tears already beginning to stream from his face. "I just can't do it."

"I can," said Luke, as he lay the gun on the fort's windowsill, quickly took aim, and fired.

The bullet hit the man in his right calf. He screamed, and Luke fumbled trying to get another bullet chambered. He had the magazine out, but bobbled the round and dropped it onto the floor of the fort. Finally, his fingers found it, and with shaking hands, he slid the bullet into the magazine. "They're gone," said Scott flatly, and when Luke looked up he saw that it was true. Rain was falling heavily now among the trees, and there was no sign of them. It was as if they'd never been there at all.

"We need to get this gun back to my house," said Scott. "And then we need to call the police." He looked for the empty brass on the floor of the fort, but gave up quickly—it could have been any-where. "Now, we need to go now!"

19

Hooper felt the bullet before he heard it. It was a sharp, stinging pain, and when it was followed by the distinctive crack of a rifle, he was immediately sure that he'd been shot. He screamed, bellowing with everything he had in his body, but the worst part wasn't the pain, it was the look on her face. Amy was smiling. She looked beautiful, utterly vivacious and full of life, so happy to see him suffering. *I'll remember this, you little bitch.*

Hooper staggered from the pain, then got his legs back under him and forced himself to fight the instinct to look for where the shot had come from. Instead, he bit into his cheek, hard, pushed the gun harder into her back, and moved her into thicker brush, popples, brambles, and prickers.

It wasn't a direct line to the house, not anymore, but Hooper figured that was OK. Someone had seen him, and known that what was happening was bad enough to risk shooting at an armed man. Hooper wished he could see who'd done it and kill him, shoot him in the stomach and watch him die like a dog. Did he understand the lengths Hooper had gone to get Amy, to keep her? Why would anyone want to take something away from a stranger? Hooper understood the risks law enforcement, posed but hated to imagine the kind of person who would try and take someone like Amy away from him. He had, after all, already lost her once.

Once they were hidden among the trees, Hooper took a minute to listen. It would have been easy for someone to have pursued them to this point, but the brush they were in now was thick enough that no one was going to be able to just sneak up on them. He gave a look to his leg, leaving the gun pointed at Amy's back. There was a little hole in his jeans, and he was bleeding, but not much, at least not yet. Not ready to see the hole, Hooper pulled the front of his pant leg up, hoping to see that the bullet had passed through, and winced when he saw that it hadn't. *That's not good.*

Knowing that he needed to ignore the pain, both present and yet to come, Hooper pushed the pistol into her back, hard. Amy arched away from the gun, and Hooper said, "Move." She did.

They came out of the popples after a few hundred feet of walking through the tightly wound brush. Hooper could see the burrs all over Amy, but didn't care like he should have. Bile was churning in his stomach, and nausea swept through him as he walked. Rain was pouring over them, and there might have been thunder, but he wasn't sure. When he finally saw the row of houses as the trees began to give way to civilization, he ground the barrel of the pistol into Amy's back, as though trying to share some of the pain from his leg. "If you yell or try to run, I will shoot you." She didn't say anything, just kept walking ahead of him with the gun in her back.

They finally made the fence, just as a tremendous roar of thunder made Hooper think for an instant he was being shot at again. He stumbled, and for a second he felt like she might run, but the moment passed. They crossed through the fence, and Hooper shut the gate behind him. The small amount of strength and energy he had left was fading; he wanted to collapse on the lawn and just sleep for a few days. He knew that was impossible, though. As much as he hated the idea of going to jail, he hated the idea of losing Amy even more. That thought was enough to fuel him to herd her like livestock into the house.

He needed to get her into the basement and himself looking normal again. It was possible the person who had shot him had recognized him, but Hooper thought he looked too nondescript for that to happen. Either way, though, the cops were going to be here soon, that was pretty much a guarantee. Hooper slammed the sliding door shut behind him, then locked it and dropped the blinds closed.

20

Scott set the rifle back where he'd found it in Carl's room in the basement, gave one more look around to make sure there was no other sign that he'd been in there, then shut off the light and headed upstairs. Tim was lying on the floor with a wet towel on his forehead, still looking like he might pass out. Luke wasn't doing much better. He was sitting at the kitchen table wearing a thousand-yard stare. "You guys need to snap out of it," said Scott. "Like, right now. I'm going to call the cops."

They had run from the fort, not considering what would have happened if the man who had been with Molly had been laid up and waiting for them. He hadn't been, though. By the time they burst from the woods and back onto Scott's street, the rain had turned from a summer shower to a full-on thunderstorm. Lightning crackled in the sky, and thunder rumbled. Scott unlocked the door, and they had made it into the house when Tim's knees buckled. "You have to help him," Scott said to Luke, running on to the kitchen to get a towel to dry the gun, and then booking it downstairs.

"We have to tell the cops that I shot him," Luke said now, flatly. "If we don't, they're going to figure it out later, and I'm going to get in a ton of trouble. I shot him. Holy shit, I shot a pers—"

"Shut up," said Scott. "I understand that you guys are freaked out, and I am too, but we need to get our story straight, and it can't involve the rifle."

Luke and Tim, who was propped up on one elbow now, stared at him.

"If this guy gets caught," Scott said, "and if they pull a bullet out of him, then we admit to it. No one will think it was a big deal because a bad guy got caught. If we say we did it before he gets caught, though, we're just admitting that we shot someone. And *we* shot him, Luke, not just you. We did it." Scott took a deep breath, and then continued.

"I'm going to call the cop that I talked to, and then you guys are going to call your parents, and I'm going to call my mom at work. The story we're going to tell is simple: we tell them everything that happened except for the part about the gun. All the rest of it's fine: we were up in the fort shooting air rifles and—"

"Luke and I don't have our air rifles with us," said Tim. "If that cop that Scott talked to is the same one that was at my house, he's going to be able to see through our lies really easily. He made me feel like I'd done something wrong without even talking to me."

Luke nodded in agreement and said, "We'll just say we were all shooting your air rifle, Scott. That works. And it's really close to the truth."

"I'm going to call him now," said Scott. "Remember what I said." Scott dug the card from his pocket, then took the phone off of the cradle and spun the number in. He held the phone to his ear, and someone said, "Van Endel."

"Is this Detective Van Endel?"

"This is he. Can I help you?" The detective sounded busy, gruff, and Scott could already feel fear rushing through his veins like fire. "Uhh, yeah," said Scott. "My name's Scott Dijkstra, and I talked to you yesterday. I was the kid you saw with muddy shoes. My friends and I think we saw Molly Peterson with a man. He had a gun."

"Where are you now?"

"At home, 229 Fernwood. Right where you saw me yesterday."

"Are your friends with you?"

"Yes."

"All right. You need to lock all the doors in the house and turn out the lights. I'm going to put this through to Emergency and get a squad car out there as soon as possible. Hang on." Scott could hear Van Endel screaming something, but it was muffled, as though the mouthpiece on the other end had been palmed. Then Van Endel was talking to him again. "Do you know if you were seen?"

"No," said Scott, then remembered the bullet in the man's leg. *He had to have known someone was out there with him and Molly.* "Well, maybe. I don't think he saw us leave the woods, though."

"All right," said Van Endel. Scott could hear stress in the man's voice, and didn't think that was a good thing. "Here's what I want you to do. Have you locked those doors and turned out the lights?"

"No, not—"

"Have your buddies do it. Now." When Scott had told Tim and Luke and they'd run off, Van Endel went on. "I'm going to hang up, and I want you to call 911. Let them know where you are, that you spoke to me, and that a car has already been dispatched and should be there any minute. They will verify that the officer is at your location when he gets there. Do not let anyone in the house until you are told by the 911 operator that an officer is on your porch. And stay away from the windows."

"My friends here need to call their parents," said Scott.

"That's going to have to wait a few minutes. I'm going to hang up now so I can get ready to meet you when you come down here. Do you have any questions?"

"No."

The phone clicked and turned to a dial tone. Scott pushed the button to hang up, and then slowly dialed 911. His friends were back with him and watched while he dialed. His hand was shaking as it worked the wheel, and he wondered why it had taken so long for him to realize that they could be in danger.

———

It was less than ten minutes later when the 911 operator named Carol said that it was OK to open the front door. Nothing had happened in the ten minutes since Scott had first dialed Van Endel until now, and he figured that was a good thing. By the tone of relief in Carol's voice when she said that an officer was at his house, Scott could tell that she did too. He thanked her and hung up the phone, then walked to the door and slowly opened it.

A police officer was there, with his back to him. He was holding a shotgun. Without looking back, the officer said, "Go ahead and get it all the way open, son. I'm going to back in."

Scott did as the man asked, pulling the door open as far as it would go, and then backing up as the cop methodically walked backward into his house, before slamming the door. Only then did the cop turn around. He was older, older than Carl; if he'd had to guess, Scott would have guessed he was fifty, maybe older. "Are you guys all OK?" he asked, and the boys nodded. "OK, good, really good." He gestured with a wave to the kitchen. "Let's go on and get away from the front door, all right?"

None of them said anything in response, they just walked where the officer told them to and he followed them into the kitchen. "I'm Officer Summers," said the cop. "And we'll have this thing stabilized soon. Right now we just need to hang tight until that happens. Sound good?"

"Sure," said Tim, the first words he'd spoken since getting off of the floor. "Can we call our parents yet, though?"

Officer Summers silenced a suddenly squealing walkie-talkie, then responded, saying, "Let's just wait for some more cops to get here, OK, guys?"

21

"Here's what we got," said Van Endel to Dr. Martinez. She'd come across town to the station in record time, and he owed her massively for rushing, not to mention whatever damage she might be doing to her private practice, but didn't care at the moment. The age he'd been given for all three of the boys who had seen Molly with her abductor was twelve. Grilling suspects and adult victims and witnesses was one thing. He'd need Martinez there to help extract every little bit of information they could out of the kids.

Van Endel and Martinez were in a room with three telephones, all with separate lines, along a mirrored glass window. There were two other rooms like this in the station, all of them bordering the interrogation rooms. There was also a pair of televisions in the room, and they showed what was happening in the two rooms besides this; everything always recorded by cameras. For Van Endel, being in there felt almost like the locker room had before his knee chased him away from hockey for the last time. Getting a confession from a suspect meant a hell of a lot more than winning at some game did, though.

"Three twelve-year-olds were playing in a tree house," Van Endel began, "when they saw two people walking in the woods.

One of them was a girl matching the description of Molly, the other one was an adult male with a gun. As soon as the two were out of sight, the boys ran off and got to a phone, then called 911."

"They got lucky," said Dr. Martinez. "Whoever he is, I'm sure he'd have no problem killing to keep his secret safe."

"I was thinking the same thing," said Van Endel. "Why are you giving me that look?"

"Because you already think they might be lying," said Dr. Martinez, "and that's something you need to stop doing right now. These kids could be the first break in this thing that we've had. Hopefully they can provide us with some solid information, and we can get everything settled. The mere fact that she's alive is great news all on its own."

"She *was* still alive. According to three kids in a tree house. We'll see what they can tell us, but don't go getting your hopes up. They're just kids, and what they think they saw could be very different from what they actually saw. In fact, I'd be willing to bet—"

"You can't afford to think that way. We can't afford to close our minds to—"

"I'm just telling you. How many dead ends—"

"And I'm telling you, you need to lighten up," said Dr. Martinez. "Take some time off, go on some dates. Spread your wings and fly, Dick. Trust me, I know."

"You got any prospects for me?" Van Endel asked with a weary smile. "Any nubile gym rats such as yourself that haven't shunned men?"

"Detective, even if I did have any, I wouldn't tell you. I meet somebody like that, she's all mine." She smiled. "Better."

"What?"

"The look on your face. It's a little better. Seriously, though, Dick, keep an open mind, and stay calm. These kids are probably scared out of their minds already; the last thing they're going to react well to is a detective they perceive as badgering them. And believe me, their parents won't like it any better. Keep cool, and if

I start to lead a conversation, let me. You're a good cop, but I know kids. Let me do my job, you do yours, and maybe this thing will have a happy ending after all."

Van Endel spared a look at his watch. *What in the hell is taking so long?* He took a deep breath and let it out. He knew exactly what was taking so long: that whole area was getting secured by uniforms. For all they knew, there really was a man with a gun on the loose in the suburbs.

Van Endel and Dr. Martinez snapped their heads around as the door to the room opened. "They're en route," said Don, before shutting the door behind him.

22

"Pick up that bag," said Hooper, pointing at the brown sack from the fuck store. She scurried over to it and Hooper followed, slowly. He locked the front door, and when he turned she'd swung the bag back over her shoulder like she was winding up to hit him with it. "What the fuck?" he said. "Just carry the damn thing down the stairs, now." She sagged and walked in front of him and began to descend the steps.

Hooper followed her. He was soaking wet from the forest, and felt cold, but sweat was pouring off of him, and he could feel blood running down his leg. Four steps down the stairway, with Amy just ahead of him, Hooper tripped as his leg went dead. He dropped through the air, crashing on top of Amy, and the two of them slid down the rest of the steps together and landed on the basement floor.

The next few seconds felt like forever to Hooper. Amy standing first, the 1911 in her shaking hands, the barrel huge and pointed at his face. Next, his arm wrapped around her leg, yanking it and sending her hurtling to the floor. Then he was climbing over her body, fighting with her for a few seconds before recovering the gun.

The world came back into focus then, with Amy sitting before him and him back on his feet, the gun in his hand, steady. He picked up the bag from the fuck store and dumped out the contents before her, her eyes bulging at what was inside.

"Take off those clothes," he said. "Do it right now—you've worn out all of my patience."

Amy got to her feet and stripped out of the wet and ill-fitting clothing, leaving the lumpy pile of shirt and shorts sitting on the basement floor. Hooper couldn't help but look at her body for a second, before reminding himself that time was finite. As if to highlight this, Hooper could hear sirens. *I never unloaded the car. If they look in it I'm fucked.*

He pushed the bad thought aside. One thing after the other, that was how it had to be. He kicked at the ball gag. "Put it on now." She did, but too slowly, and Hooper punched the gun into her stomach, hard. She doubled up and then stood, the ball in place, her eyes watering.

"Sit against that pole," said Hooper, pointing at the pole where he had first secured her with rope. She did, and Hooper kicked the handcuffs behind her. He set the 1911 down and fastened the handcuffs on her wrists one after the other, behind the pole and as tight as they could go. Finally, with her somewhat secure, Hooper tucked the gun into his waistband.

He bound her legs together with the longer, chained cuffs meant for ankles, and placed the collar around her neck. "They might come to the door, and you can try and yell and make all the noise you want. If you do, however, I'm going to shoot the cop, come down here and fuck you, slit your throat, and then kill myself. Do you understand?"

She nodded, eyes wide. *She'll be docile as a lamb once the last little bit of fight is out of her,* Hooper thought as he shut off the light and went up the stairs.

The first thing to do was get rid of the restraints she'd broken free from, and it took Hooper all of about five seconds to see how she'd gotten out. He knew the kitchen chairs were old, but it looked like all she'd had to do was tip over, and the thing had come apart into five or six pieces. It had to have happened right before he'd walked in, thank God. She'd only had time to put on the clothes he'd left in the hamper from the day before, and then walk to the slider to escape. Hooper guessed she'd been free for maybe sixty seconds, maximum, when he'd walked into the house. It didn't get much closer than that. Hooper filled his arms with chair, straps, and rope and walked to the attached garage.

The garage door was still open, the garage lights blazing. The surprise of the light shocked Hooper. He felt like an idiot. Of course it was open—he had walked in through the front of the house. He dropped the mess of wood and bindings by the trash, then walked to the door and closed it quickly, so that it bounced once on the pavement before settling. With a look over his shoulder at the boards in the car, Hooper left to get the rest of the ruined chair.

Once it was all in the garage—the noise of sirens getting louder and more constant—Hooper walked to the bedroom and finally stripped off the wet clothes. He was considering the bathroom when a knock at the door made his blood run cold. He jumped into a pair of jeans, attempted to quickly dry his still-wet hair with a towel, and walked to the door clad in only blue jeans, the 1911 stuck in the back of his pants.

He answered the door casually, trying to look a little shocked when he saw the cop. "What's going on, Officer?" Hooper asked the guy in the uniform, a man about his own age, wearing sunglasses despite the dark clouds, as well as a thick mustache.

"We're looking for this girl," said the cop, who held out a school picture of Amy for him. "She went missing a couple of days ago from the drive-in, and we just got a report that someone saw her in the woods behind your house with a white male."

The drive-in. Her friends are still telling the lie, Hooper thought with suppressed joy. If she hadn't tried to escape, he'd be in the clear. "I haven't seen her, Officer," said Hooper, hoping he hadn't botched things with his delayed response.

"I'm not surprised to hear that, Mr.—"

"Hooper. Matt Hooper. And I'm glad you're not surprised, but can I ask why? I'm a white male. I live alone here. I'm sure you fellas want to find that girl in your picture."

The cop pointed to Hooper's chest, to the tattoo he'd gotten in Saigon of a bulldog's head with a banner, holding the number 1969. "I was there a year or so after you were, Mr. Hooper. Lost some good friends over there."

"I hear that," said Hooper. His knee was starting to shake, and Hooper could feel blood pooling under his foot. If the cop had placed his hand on his chest and shoved, Hooper would have fallen over like a stack of bricks.

But the cop just grinned. "Well, I'm going to get back to looking for bad guys, Mr. Hooper," he said. "Probably a snipe hunt, but you never know. Have yourself a nice afternoon."

"You too, Officer," said Hooper, before the cop turned and Hooper shut the door. He slipped the lock, took two steps by dragging his hurt leg, and then collapsed to the floor, shaking violently.

23

Tim, Scott, and Luke were driven to the police station in the back of a squad car. Uniformed cops were scurrying about like overweight relatives at an all-you-can-eat buffet. They were visibly shaken, walking through yards with guns out, talking to other possible witnesses, and generally disrupting a summer afternoon in the worst possible way. It had stopped raining by the time the boys left the house, but the streets and sidewalks were still wet. Once they were at the police station, the three boys were led out of the car, past the lobby, and to a small room with a mirror and no window. Officer Summers gave them a wave when he left them, and Detective Van Endel entered the room before the door could swing shut, along with a woman wearing a suit.

"All right, guys," said Van Endel. "Just so we're all formally introduced, I'm Detective Van Endel, and this is Dr. Martinez. She's a children's therapist that I've worked with for a long time, and she's here to talk to you because she's the best, and I all but begged her to get down here. Before we start, I want you to know that we were able to get ahold of Tim and Scott's parents. Luke, one of the officers spoke to your sister Alisha, and she said she can get your mom. Sounds like she's with friends. Now, the point of me telling you this is that I need to talk to you guys, but I'm not supposed to do that without a parent here." Another officer opened the door, interrupting Van Endel, and then set a VHS camcorder on a tripod down in front of them. "It's all set for you, Detective," said the other cop before leaving.

"As I was saying," said Van Endel, "I'm bending the rules talking to you guys right now, but according to what Scott said on the phone, you guys saw Molly Peterson with a gun in her back, being forcibly taken through the woods. Because time is so important in this sort of situation, I need to talk to you guys about some small details to help out the police on the scene, and then when your folks get here we can go over the details." Van Endel grimaced, as though the next part were particularly distasteful. "But if you guys are going to help me, I need to videotape the whole thing, and I need to ask you if you're willing to talk to me, also on tape. So if you guys feel comfortable, and you're willing to say as much on tape, we can start looking for Molly that much sooner."

"We'll do it," said Tim. "I know I will, anyways. Molly needs our help."

Van Endel nodded, then stood. "You guys in too?" Scott and Luke both said yes at the same time. "OK, then," said Van Endel, who removed a lens cap, then pushed a button on the camera, making a red light come on below the lens. "I'm Detective Richard Van Endel, here with Dr. Andrea Martinez, and the reason we're recording this is so we have a record showing that the young men we're talking to were not coerced into talking with us. Am I correct in stating that you want to discuss this matter, gentlemen?"

"Yes."

"Yes."

"Yes."

"All right, excellent. What did you guys see on the state land behind your houses?"

Tim, Scott, and Luke exchanged a look, and Tim said, "We were in the fort that we built, just screwing around with Scott's air rifle, when Luke saw Molly walking in the woods. We all looked where he was pointing, and we saw Molly walking with a guy right behind her. They were super close together. When they got closer, we could see that he had a gun."

"Where is this fort?"

"In the middle of three pines. We built it out of some old deck wood. My dad's putting in a patio."

"All right. Will my officers have trouble finding it?"

"No," said Luke. "They shouldn't."

"I'll get some paper in a minute, and you can try and draw me a map. What direction were you facing when you saw her?"

"South," said Scott. "They came from the south, and then walked west. We lost sight of them in the trees up there. They were moving pretty quickly, and we were all pretty freaked out about being seen."

"And that would have been closest to your house, Scott?" Dr. Martinez asked with a smile.

"Sort of, kind of between the different ways that Tim and I would walk home."

"And that was the last you saw of them?"

"Yes," said Scott, and Tim and Luke nodded. "Then it started raining and that was it. They were gone." Van Endel turned off the record button. "All right, thanks, guys. That'll get us a good enough start on the search. I'm going to need to speak to you all again once your parents get here, and some of that might get stressful as we go over the finer details, especially if we don't have anyone in custody yet, but I want you to know that I really appreciate how brave you guys have been so far, and we'll be back soon."

———

Tim was sitting alone in an interrogation room when his mom burst in and nearly bowled him over in an enthusiastic embrace. Then she pushed him away and inspected him for damage.

Finding none, she said, "What happened? I want every detail. Have they been nice to you? They told us one of the detectives had to interview you before we were here, and if he did anything wrong, I want to know about it." Tim smiled at her, and then at his dad, who had entered the room behind her. "It's fine, you guys. Detective Van Endel has been really nice, and there's a doctor lady too, she—"

"I knew it!" Tammy said. "I knew that's who they were going to have talking to them. We are going to watch that tape, Stanley. They're crazy if they think I'm not calling my lawyer the second we get out of here."

"Tammy," said Stan. "Calm down. Tim is doing fine. Let's see what the detective has to say, and we'll go from there. Does that sound good, Tim?"

"That sounds fine, and, Mom, Dad's right. Detective Van Endel and Dr. Martinez were really nice. We were the ones who called *them*, remember. They have to ask us questions. They only talked to us so that they had a better chance of helping Molly and catching the guy who kidnapped her. I just hope she's OK. Do they know anything yet?"

"Not that we know of," said Stan. "But that's what everyone is hoping, that she gets home safe and sound. She got darn lucky you guys built that fort. You've never spent so much time in the woods before. I'm just glad that guy didn't see you. If he did, it could have been really bad."

"Yeah," said Tim, trying to keep his composure. *Get it together. If this was Van Endel, he'd know you were lying about something.* "I'm just hopeful, if he did see us, that all he saw was some dumb old tree fort."

The door opened, and Van Endel walked in with the doctor. Van Endel shook hands with Tim's parents, then said, "This is Dr. Martinez. She's a children's therapist who assists us when we need to talk to children who have been through some sort of trauma."

She shook all of their hands, one after the other, even Tim's, and then sat next to the detective. "I know Tim's not hurt physically, and that all three of the boys seem to be doing fine," she said. "I'm just here to make sure everyone is doing as well as they say they are."

"We're glad to have you, Dr. Martinez," said Tammy, but all of a sudden, Tim wasn't sure he was glad at all. Was she really here for him, or for Van Endel? Was he worried they were going to lie, or convinced that they already had been?

"I'm going to be recording everything we say," said Van Endel. "Just in case any of this gets used in court, we'll have an early template to work with." He laid a tape recorder on the table and hit record. "Detective Van Endel," he said. "July first, 1987, eleven o'clock a.m., speaking with Tim Benchley and his parents, Tammy and Stanley Benchley. Tim, why don't we start with everything you remember, starting with what happened right before you saw Molly and the man."

"All right," said Tim. "Luke, Scott, and I were sitting in the tree fort we built. We were shooting Scott's air rifle and arguing a little bit over taking turns." He smiled. "We all have one, but neither Luke or I brought ours with us today. No real reason why, we just didn't. Anyways, I was about to shoot at a target when Luke told me to stop. Then he pointed at Molly and a guy walking behind her, only really closely. Molly looked really upset, and when they were close to us—"

"How close, Tim?" Van Endel asked. "Do your best to estimate, but if you're not sure, just say you're not sure, OK?"

"All right. I guess we were about…fifty feet away from them when they stopped, then turned and started walking away from us—"

"What direction?"

"West, they went west, and then they were just gone."

"What was Molly wearing?"

"Huh?"

"When you saw Molly, how was she dressed? Were her clothes clean or dirty? Did she look as though she were dressed to go out with friends, or was she wearing everyday clothes?"

"I don't know. She was just dressed regular, I guess. Neither of them was wearing anything that really stuck out, just clothing."

Van Endel and Dr. Martinez shared a glance. Either Tim wasn't supposed to notice or maybe it was meant to unsettle him. *They don't trust me, but I'm telling the truth.*

"Tim," said Dr. Martinez, "I want you to close your eyes and picture Molly exactly as she was a few hours ago. Try to make a picture of her in your mind, and describe the picture to us."

"OK," said Tim, his voice cracking slightly. He took a deep breath, then really tried to picture her. All that was coming was the rifle sights, and a stark image of the man screaming after being shot by Luke. Molly's clothes weren't there, she could have been wearing a ball gown for all Tim remembered.

Sensing his frustration, or perhaps further probing him for information, Dr. Martinez said, "We know that this is going to be tough, Tim. But the thing is, we need you and your friends to help. Every little detail you can tell us, even a silly thing like what she was wearing, that stuff can help make a difference. I need you to concentrate and really think, OK?"

"I am," said Tim. He felt sick, and wondered if they could tell. It wasn't like he'd felt in Scott's house right after it had happened, but it was almost as bad. *If I puke, will they let me go?* He knew they wouldn't, though; that might just lead to more questions. Finally, trying to get them off his back, and with his eyes squarely on the tape recorder, Tim said, "She wasn't wearing anything that stuck out to me. Maybe it was just a shirt and shorts. I really don't know."

Van Endel made a notepad appear in his hand from his pocket, then started flipping through it. Finally he stopped, tapping a finger on a page of the notebook. He smiled at Tim, an "aha" look in his eyes. "I've got it right here, from my conversation with Mrs.

Peterson, Molly's mom. She said that when she left the house at around six o'clock p.m. two nights ago, Molly was heavily made up in the face and was wearing a neon-pink pencil skirt, along with a shirt that hung off of one shoulder and said RATT. Does that sound like the regular clothes she was wearing this morning to you?"

"No," said Tim. "It doesn't sound like what she was wearing at all."

"My notes with Mrs. Peterson also tell us a little bit about Molly's hair," said Van Endel. "I know that it was poufed up like some of the girls do these days. Did it look like that, or maybe like a hairdo like that might look after a couple days with no attention paid to it? Matted, maybe, or wild?"

"I know it was Molly," said Tim. "But not because of her hair or her clothes—I knew it was her because of her face."

"Can you describe the face of the man she was with?"

"Detective," said Tammy. "My son is clearly terrified. He saw a kidnapped girl this morning, and now he's being made to feel as though he's done something wrong. I would really appreciate if you'd back off on the tone a little bit. This is a twelve-year-old boy you're talking to."

"Ma'am, I apologize if my tone seems harsh," said Van Endel. "But there is a missing girl out there, and your son and his friends were the last people to see her. Any bit of information I can get from them could wind up being the piece of this puzzle that sees Molly go home to her family. Your daughter, I know I have her name in my notes—"

"Rebecca," said Stan.

"Yes, Rebecca. If she was the one missing and some boys claimed to have seen her being forcibly transported with a gun in her back, would you feel badly if my tone offended one of those boys? We're going to take a break, and the doc and I are going to talk to one of the other boys. If you could, please impress on your son how important it is that he recall, in great detail if possible, the events of this morning."

Van Endel stood with Dr. Martinez, and he paused the tape recorder. He ejected the tape and tucked it in his pocket, and they opened the door and left.

"They're acting like he's some criminal," hissed Tammy. "Tim didn't do anything wrong, nothing, and they're acting like he's the one breaking the law. We need to get him out of here and then call a lawyer. They can't treat us like this!"

"Tammy, you need to calm down," said Stan, his voiced muted and dull. "And, Tim, you need to try harder. These people are just trying to do their jobs." Tammy raised a hand to her mouth. She looked like she might get sick. *Dad doesn't believe me either. I sure hope Scott and Luke do a better job than I did.*

24

Scott sat next to his mom. Carl had offered to come, but Beth told him that she didn't think Carl needed to miss his first day of training for his new position. When the detective and doctor came into the room and introduced themselves to Scott's mom, Scott realized that he hadn't even had the chance to tell her what had happened. Van Endel set a tape recorder on the desk, said something about the date, along with their names, then cleared his throat.

"How are you doing, Scott?" Van Endel asked.

"I'm doing OK. Still a little freaked out, but OK, I guess," Scott said, trying to feel confident, but each word slipped from his mouth as though it were steeped in syrup.

"I want you to tell me everything you remember," said Van Endel. Behind him, Dr. Martinez was smiling thinly and nodding. "Just go over all of it, all right? Let's start with an easy one: How was she dressed? Try and make us feel like we're right there with you."

"All right. I guess I'd say she was wearing normal clothes for a hot day." As soon as the words escaped his lips, Scott knew somehow, something was wrong. Dr. Martinez had immediately looked at Van Endel, the sort of glance he wasn't supposed to notice but had anyway.

"Could you clarify for us, son?" Van Endel said it with a smile on his face, but already, Scott didn't trust the detective he'd been so excited to have met just a short time ago. "We really need a more definitive idea of how she looked. Was she hurt?"

"No, I don't think she was hurt. She looked really, really scared, though."

"I'm sure she did," said Van Endel. "But what I want to know is what she was wearing, Scott."

"She was wearing…" Scott stumbled over the words, his face reddening instantly. "I don't know, I don't want to be wrong. I didn't really notice her clothes. They were just clothes, hot-day stuff."

"I'd rather you be wrong, and still hear a definitive guess," said Van Endel. "Hearing you say 'just clothes,' that doesn't tell me anything. I want something I can get my teeth in, do you understand?"

Dr. Martinez leaned forward. "Scott, let's just relax. A lot of times, we see more than we really think we do. Try taking a deep breath, maybe closing your eyes, and—"

"Can I ask what the problem is?" Scott's mom asked in an annoyed tone, the one Carl called her uptown voice. "You called me in from work for this, and my son has tried to answer this silly question. It matters what she was wearing? You're in trouble if it does. A twelve-year-old boy is going to notice a girl's clothes? These boys are lucky if their socks match. Scott said he saw a man holding a gun on a kidnapped girl, isn't that more important than what the girl looked like? What am I missing here?"

Van Endel and Dr. Martinez shared a look, and Van Endel said, "Ma'am," when a knock on the door interrupted him. "Excuse me," he continued, barely missing a beat. "Why don't you come too, Doc? This will give Scott a chance to think and talk to his mom."

"What is it?" Van Endel said as he opened the door. "We're in there trying to figure out where—" Then it was shut behind him and Dr. Martinez and his voice was gone.

"Why don't they believe me?" Scott asked his mom, once he was sure the door was all the way closed. "All they're doing is asking me about her stupid clothes, and I'm telling the truth, but they still don't believe me."

"Calm down," she said. "I think they're just trying to verify that you aren't making any of this up. It's their job to be distrustful; it might be the reason they wound up working here in the first place." She sighed. "Either way, just keep your chin up. Hey, wasn't Carl's news the best? I can't wait to cash out my last table."

"You could just quit, Mom. You don't owe them anything."

She shook her head. "No way. That would totally mess up the schedule and make everyone else have to pick up other shifts. I kind of feel bad about quitting as it is. Isn't that weird? All I've done is complain for years about that place, and now I don't want to leave, in this really weird way."

25

Van Endel was furious. He was in there trying to figure this shit out, which was bad enough, and now Summers was pulling him out of an interrogation. Walt knew better. This was beyond unprofessional—it could ruin the minor progress that he and Dr. Martinez had made. Van Endel was ready to scream, thought maybe he was already screaming, when he saw Chief Sanborn standing next to a wounded-looking Walt.

"My office, now," said Chief Jefferson flatly, and Van Endel took Walt's nod as he entered the office as a mark of sympathy.

This is bad, I know it.

Chief Jefferson sat behind his desk after waddling around it, then turned on Van Endel with an annoyed look. "Stretch out your drumsticks, and sit down. I got bad news, and you're not going to like it, so let's get it over with."

Van Endel sat reluctantly. The chief and he had been at odds for almost six months over Van Endel's handling of the Riverside business. Van Endel was a smart enough man to know that his attitude hadn't helped. Regrettably, and especially to his boss, neither had his detective work. Van Endel grinned, then frowned, but got no reaction. Finally, he took a Werther's Original from a bowl on Jefferson's desk and said, "Spill it."

"We got a body," said Jefferson. "White female, burned beyond recognition, teeth smashed out with a hammer. Whoever does dental on this girl is going to be in for a serious nightmare."

"Where was she?" Van Endel asked, his voice higher than normal, pulse accelerating. "How long has she been deceased?" He looked at the clock on the wall. The 911 call was less than ninety minutes old.

"Calm down," said Jefferson. "I see that look in your eyes, but it's not what you think. She's been dead about two days, according to the coroner, and from the amount of fire damage, she burned for a while." Jefferson lit a cigarette, coughed twice into a handkerchief, then leaned back in his chair. "Body was found in a shallow grave, near the drive-in but off the property. You need to go down and talk to the guys working that night, get the fear of God into them, maybe even give them a serious look as possible suspects."

"So the whole 911 call was bullshit?" Van Endel asked, in a voice that was escalating now. He could feel rage boiling in his stomach. *If that was my fucking kid and he did that...*Van Endel let out a breath he'd been unconsciously holding in.

"Yep," said Jefferson. "That seems pretty damned obvious. You're going to go back in there, and you're going to very politely tell those kids that they're a bunch of fuckin' attention-seeking, miserable little pricks, and then you're going to go the crime scene. If that sounds like an order, it's because it is. The coroner is saying the body is close to the height and weight of the Peterson girl, so after you're done at the crime scene, you're going to the morgue with the body to verify, eyes-on, that those things are correct."

"Have you contacted the mother yet?"

"Nope, not yet," said Jefferson. "That's next, just as soon as your butt's out of that chair. I'm going to call the mother, give her a heads-up on the possibility of really bad news, and then when you verify the size of our corpse, I'll let her know we're waiting on dental."

"How long do you think dental will take? I know normally it's only a few days, but is it even possible when the teeth are that bad?"

"Doesn't matter, dental's going to come up positive," said Jefferson. "The press is going to report this kid is dead, so is the TV news. It's going to be all over. Even if dental does come back negative, it won't be worth a shit. The guy from the coroner's office, the new whiz kid they got, he says the perp stabbed her to death, then meticulously—his word—pulped out her fucking teeth before burning her. We won't get within a mile of conclusive with the girl's damn teeth.

"Back to those fucking kids. This is some malicious, deliberate shit, and those little assholes need to know that playtime is over. Then it's time to kick in some doors and find this fucker."

"I'm on it," said Van Endel, standing. He was walking out the door when Jefferson called after him, "Don't fuck this up. This girl isn't some whore. She's one of us." Van Endel wanted to shout back at Jefferson and tell him that response was precisely why they were nowhere on the Riverside case. If the prostitute murders had been treated with this sort of priority, it could have been solved long ago. There was no point. Van Endel let the door chase him out, and then his eyes were on Dr. Martinez. He crossed the room quickly to her.

"Well?" said Dr. Martinez in a hushed voice. "What was so damn important?"

"They got a body," said Van Endel, his voice just as quiet.

"Oh, my God," she said, the color draining from her face. "Where, in the woods? I feel so terrible; if only we could have done more, or had a little bit more time. Fucking shit, seriou—"

"Doc, you need to calm down right now," said Van Endel, grabbing her arm. "They found her at the drive-in, and she's a burned-up wreck, and been there two days or so. Those kids didn't see shit in those woods except for maybe some squirrels."

"I can't believe this," said Dr. Martinez. "They were acting scared and a little unsure of themselves, but I thought with time and some hard work we were going to get somewhere. Are they sure it's her?"

"Pretty damn sure," said Van Endel. "I have to tell these kids to get the fuck out, and then I'm going to the drive-in, and then the morgue. Want to come?"

"Wouldn't miss it," said Martinez, her face a stone.

26

The door opened, and both Scott's and Beth's heads snapped toward it. Van Endel walked in first. He looked furious. Dr. Martinez followed, not looking a whole lot happier. "There is a very good chance that Molly is deceased," said Van Endel. "A body has been found."

"Oh, my God, how awful," Scott's mom said. "Her poor mother."

Van Endel was pacing the small room back and forth. "Agreed," he said. "Her poor mother. But we have a problem. A big one. The medical examiner is pretty sure that the girl we found has been dead for a couple of days, likely the same day she was taken. The body's pretty badly burned, but he'll know exactly how long soon enough."

"That's not possible!" Scott nearly shouted. "We just saw her, and she was alive. It's been like two or three hours, tops, and most of that was spent waiting to talk to you!"

"Young man," said Van Endel, "I am going to say this one time, and one time only. Calm down. Right now. My boss has it in his head that you kids are lying, and I'm starting to agree with him. As I said, we still need to verify details, but it seems highly likely that the body recovered is Molly, and if that's the case—"

"Mom, this is crazy! We saw Molly, and if someone would just lis—"

"Scott," his mom said, "you need to shut your mouth, OK?" Scott couldn't believe it, but it was happening. She wasn't even looking at him. "Detective, Doctor, I'm so sorry. I'm not sure what he was thinking, but we'll get to the bottom of it. I'm so sorry we wasted your time. I honestly don't know what else to say to you."

"I get that. I'm not the only cop that's been working a lot of unpaid overtime on this one. We really wanted to bring Molly home safely, and this prank, if that's what it is, is just a slap in the face."

"I understand completely," said Scott's mom. "Scott has a savings account. If there are any fines, he will be working to pay them off. When can we leave?"

Van Endel looked at Dr. Martinez, and she shrugged her shoulders. "You can go now."

—

Tim sat in the back of his dad's car. Luke was across the backseat, but neither of them was looking at the other. Luke's mom had never shown, so Tim's folks were giving him a ride home. Tim had never seen his mom so pissed off, but his dad was worse. He hadn't said anything since shaking the hands of the doctor and the detective. He'd apologized to them both just before they all walked to the car. His mom had said, "I don't want you two to say one word in that car. If you can help it, don't even look at one another. Your father and I are furious with both of you, and I'd like to spend this car ride forgetting that either of you is even back there."

They dropped off Luke at the entrance to the trailer park without a word. He got out, looked like he wanted to say something, probably "Bye," or "Thanks for the ride." Instead he just shut the door and walked away.

Now the shit's going to hit the fan, Tim thought to himself, and of course, he was right.

His folks were silent for the rest of the ride, but when his dad parked the car, his mom said, "Room. Now. Your father and I need to discuss some things. And don't look at me like you want to say something. I don't want to hear a word of it."

"Tammy—"

"No, Stan. Not now. Go, Tim, I'm too mad to look at you right now. And when we come to talk to you, I highly suggest that you don't have your nose in a book. I want you sitting at your desk, not doing anything. Is that clear?" Tim nodded, an impossibly huge lump in his throat. "Then go," said his mom. "Just go."

They came for him twenty minutes later. He was sitting at his desk, doing exactly what his mom had instructed, absolutely nothing. The minutes had dragged by like hours, every second a drop of water waiting to drop, pregnant for an impossibly long amount of time. It was almost a relief when he heard a firm knock at his door.

"Come to the kitchen table," said his dad.

Tim stood, leaned back his head, and let out a deep breath. *Will it just make things worse if I argue?* He closed the door behind him gently and walked to the kitchen, to what felt like the hangman's noose.

His mom was sitting at the table with an open bottle of wine and an empty glass sitting in front of her. His dad had a beer where he was sitting. Normally Tim or Becca might have cracked a joke at a sight like that—it was just early afternoon—but today was not the day for jokes.

I need to remember that I know what I saw, and that I'm not lying. Easier said than done. Tim sat in his chair, facing them and glad that he wasn't crying or acting like a baby. The cops were wrong, but that wasn't his fault.

"First things first," said his dad. "Your mother and I are extremely disappointed that you were involved in whatever it was your friends cooked up. Lying to the police, especially about something so serious, is no laughing matter."

"But I wasn—"

His mom slapped the table, making her wine bottle and glass do a dance, and causing his dad's beer to foam over. "Let him finish," she snapped, "then let me finish, and *then* we'll listen to what you have to say. But only, and I mean this, only if you are going to tell the truth." She shrugged. "Everything you say right now sounds like bullshit." His mom lit a cigarette, something Tim hadn't seen her do in years, and drew off of it, the smoke collecting around the hanging light in the kitchen. His dad gave her a look, a not very nice one, and then continued speaking.

"Like I was saying, this is serious business, Tim. The cops could have charged both you and us for what you boys did. I'm not going to ask why; you can tell me later, when you're less indignant and give up on this notion that you can convince me that what you're claiming is somehow true. I'm just—dumbfounded that you would be a part of this. This isn't you." He pushed out a sigh. "But I guess it *is* you, or who you're trying to be, for God knows what reason. And we need to deal with it, *now*. Your summer is over, starting right now. You're going to help me put in the patio, and when that's done I'll come up with something else.

"That's one thing. Another is this: I've already spoken to Carl, and you and Scott are no longer friends for the rest of this summer, also starting right now. I'm talking *no* contact. And if it was possible to monitor your behavior at school to that degree, you can bet we'd say you'd never be friends, *period*. You're sure as hell not going to be hanging out outside of school, I can tell you that. I couldn't get ahold of Luke's mom, but same thing there, and Carl agreed, by the way. From now till school starts, you three are no longer friends. I don't want to hear a peep about it either.

"Carl and I also agreed that when his new schedule allows him some room to get time off, he and I are going to go out and tear that fort down. There's no reason for it to be up there if you guys can't use it. Do you have any questions?"

"No," Tim said, barely holding back the emotions and the tears with a mantra: *We didn't do anything wrong, and someday they will see that, and they will hate themselves for this moment. And I will fucking hate them too.*

27

Van Endel had expected the crime scene to have been horribly mishandled, but whatever unis had arrived first had done a good job of sealing it off. It was a small blessing. Tracy Vincent, the so-called whiz kid, as well as the youngest and most highly respected of the county coroners, was leaning against a tree, fastidiously eating an apple and reading a book. He was young, black, and brilliant, and how he'd moved up the ladder so quickly without making enemies was almost as amazing as his climbing it in the first place.

Van Endel and Dr. Martinez approached him. The three of them knew each other by name and by sight, but had yet to share an after-work cocktail. Tracy was known to be a bit of a loose cannon at the bar, as Van Endel had been before making detective, and he had a fear that they might get along too well. Tracy folded up the book, stuck it in the back pocket of his jeans, and walked to them, hand extended.

"Here to check out our crispy critter?" Tracy asked, a smile on his face. He shook Martinez's and then Van Endel's hand, then said, "Seriously, though, this one is going to be tough. I've got a body that's been burned about as badly as one can be, a mouth on it full of busted-out teeth, and not a whole lot else."

"Are you sure on the time of death?" Dr. Martinez asked. Van Endel could hear a hope in her voice—a hope that the boys were telling the truth after all—but that was a hope that he had left behind in the chief's office.

"Come with me," said Tracy, holding up the caution tape for them and then following after them. "Looking good, Doc. Keep hitting that gym. Just don't get rid of all of that cushion, all right?"

"Seriously, Tracy," said Dr. Martinez, annoyed even as she fought to suppress a smile. "We have to go look at a dead girl. Show some respect."

"I got respect for days, Doc," said Tracy, his smile audible in his voice. "As a matter of fact, I was respecting that a—"

"Tracy, I am not in the mood," said Martinez.

"What say we go to work now," said Van Endel, "and shut the fuck up?"

He couldn't remember the last time he'd felt so on edge about a case, and knowing why made it even worse. It wasn't normal to have more than a couple of material witnesses lying to you, and when they did, it was usually fairly easy to press on them until one of them ruptured and burst. This was different. Two groups of kids, different ages, and no associations besides the Benchley kids. Even among those two, there was no apparent angle, just a big sister and a little brother living in separate worlds.

The pit where the body lay covered in a white sheet was surrounded by prints from a German shepherd, along with boot prints from its trainer. Such things were unavoidable at a fresh crime scene.

As if reading his thoughts, Tracy said, "The other ones are mine. No one else has been in here. Which makes these fellas over here pretty goddamn interesting." Van Endel and Dr. Martinez swiveled their heads to follow his finger. There was indeed another pair of prints—boots, if Van Endel wasn't mistaken.

"I brought shit to do molds," Tracy said, "but I knew you'd blow a damn gasket if I did them before you could walk around and do all your stuff."

"I appreciate that," said Van Endel. "You had a look at the body. Our missing girl is one hundred twenty-five pounds, give or take, and she's listed at five feet, four inches. That anywhere close to a match with this girl?"

"That's where it gets tough, with this sort of barbecue. First glance, the woman in this pit figures to stand about five foot, tops, but people shrink as they burn. Think of the last time you cooked a steak."

"We get it, Tracy," said Dr. Martinez.

"Can the kitchen references, then," said Tracy, grinning. "Anyways, our girl here got cooked with an accelerant, could be gas, but I'm thinking hotter. Bones crack from that kind of heat, which further degrades our ability to nail down a positive ID. So where we're at now is, we've got a young lady who may or may not be Molly Peterson, but who most certainly was killed and burned to death roughly forty-eight hours ago, give or take about four hours."

"That seriously the best we can do?" said Van Endel.

Tracy knelt next to the sheet-covered body and slipped on a pair of white latex gloves. He removed the weights securing the blanket that covered the corpse until it would be placed in a body bag, and then pulled it from the top half of the girl.

"To be perfectly honest, Detective," said Tracy, "I think we're doing pretty fucking good with what we've been left. Once I get her to the lab, I'll be able to pin the time of death down a little closer, but sometimes, what you see is what you get."

"Poor girl," said Dr. Martinez softly under her breath, then made the sign of the cross across her chest.

Molly, or whoever it was, had been burned to almost nothing. Her skin was ash, covering not-quite-burned red flesh, along with white and yellow fat. Her eyes were gone, and her arms were folded up unnaturally, as the fire had forced her limbs to tighten. Her neck was tilted back as far as her spine would allow, her mouth open as though she were still trying to scream. The teeth were destroyed, just as Van Endel and Martinez had been told they were. *If Tracy can get an ID from those, he's even better than he says he is.* Van Endel stared death in the face for a few moments longer, and when he looked away, he saw that Dr. Martinez had turned as well.

"Cover her up," said Van Endel.

Tracy did, moving around the body deftly, taking care not to put his feet too near her. There would be time for poking and prodding later, but that was for the lab, not where she lay now.

"You see what I mean?" Tracy asked when he stood up. "That girl is gone. I'll do my best—you guys know that—but I'm not sure there's anything here to learn, aside from the fact that it was one evil motherfucker who did this to her." Two stretcher-bearing EMTs interrupted him as they walked down the path.

"I want everything you can get," said Van Endel, "even the stuff you think is nothing, all right?"

Tracy nodded, and Van Endel and Dr. Martinez made their way back up the path to the detective's car.

They were silent for the most part as they drove, Van Endel processing the day so far, and Dr. Martinez no doubt doing the same. The boys' prank had done this much good, anyway: it had launched the search that had led a police dog to the corpse. Not that they'd meant to do it, of course, but it was something, and it was far more than he'd had to go on before. It was tough to feel anything but bad about it, though. Finding the body eliminated hope completely. Molly had been found, just not the right way.

"You're going to find him, Dick," said Dr. Martinez. "You have to. I know that you feel a life is a life, and that this girl's death should be no more important than any of this bastard's other victims, and I agree with that. But the brutality of this…there was just no reason to ruin her the way he did, none at all."

"Unless we're missing something and there *is* a reason. It would hardly be a surprise at this point. Everyone else is messing with us, why not throw in a perp with motivations that are impossible to understand?"

There was something tugging at Van Endel's brain, and he let it work away while they drove to a pay phone so he could tell Chief Jefferson he was going to need to make a horrible phone call.

I'm missing something, but what?

28

Hooper woke alone, his face glued by sweat to the thick shag of the carpet in the front room. The phone was ringing in the kitchen, and he stood unsteadily to make his way to it. He tried to swallow, but his mouth felt pasted shut. He turned on the sink and sank his head into its metal bowl to drink. Finally, he pulled himself out and answered the still-ringing phone.

"Hello," said Hooper.

"Hoop? That you?" said a voice that Hooper could recognize but not place with his scrambled brain. He sat heavily on the floor, the phone teetering ominously on the counter as he sank to the ground.

"Yeah, this is Hooper. Who's this?"

"Carl, buddy. You sound like shit. Everything OK?"

Hooper smiled despite the pain in his leg and the throbbing in his head. Thank God it was just Carl. "No, I'm sicker than a dying dog. Fucking summer colds are the worst."

"You're damn straight they are. Listen, I was just calling to confirm working on the car tomorrow, but I figure you're probably not up for that."

Hooper smiled again. He'd forgotten about his plans for tomorrow completely. "No, sorry, man. I got to take a pass on that. I'll let you know when I'm better. We can hook up."

"That'd be great. My crazy stepson got into some shit today. Wait'll you hear it. It will blow your mind. I'd been feeling like he and I were the only sane ones over here, but now I'm on my own. Him and his buddies just went batshit."

"Can't wait," said Hooper, his vision blurring. What the fuck did he care about Carl's kids?

"Listen, I'm not doing anything," Carl said. "Why don't I have Beth make you up some of her famous chicken soup, and I can run it on over?"

"No," said Hooper, too quickly and too harshly. "I don't want to pass this thing around. Trust me, it's a killer." He chuckled. "Believe me, do yourself a favor and stay away from here for a day or two, all right?"

"All right, buddy," said Carl, but Hooper was still afraid his friend really thought he should stop by. *And if he does I'll probably have to kill him. He'd call an ambulance if he saw me now, and once they dig that bullet out of my leg the cops will get a warrant in no time.* "But if you change your mind," continued Carl, "let me know, OK?"

"Will do," said Hooper, before pulling the phone off of the counter onto the floor with a crash, righting the base, and then replacing the handset to disconnect the call. *Christ.*

He was thirstier and more nauseous than he'd ever been since Vietnam. He slowly pulled himself up and slid, using the counter as support, to the sink. He turned on the water and then stuck his head under the basin as he'd done the last time. The water was cold, and the shock of it against his warm skin was glorious, as was drinking oceans of it as the liquid poured from the faucet. Without removing his head from the sink, Hooper opened the cupboard closest to it and let his fingers fumble around until he'd extracted two glasses. He pulled his head free and filled them both with water, set the glasses on the counter, and then stripped off the jeans he was wearing. He suppressed a scream as they came off of his right leg, and then he shook them loose onto the floor.

With the pants off, Hooper steeled himself to finally look at his leg. Craning his head back, he could see a small black hole surrounded by blood. Coagulated blood, thick like pudding, was in and around the hole, along with a red stain that went all the way to the bottom of his foot.

Hooper limped back to the long-forgotten bags from Meijer and quickly found what he was looking for. He took the bottle of grain alcohol from the paper bag back to the kitchen, set it on the counter, and opened it. *This is going to be bad, but you have to do it.* Hooper dropped a towel on the floor, stood on it, and poured alcohol down his injured leg.

The raging fire of pain was instantaneous. It was a heat of pure white flame that seared up Hooper's leg and all through his body, consuming his very thoughts. All that there was room for in his mind was pain, but he managed to replace the bottle on the counter and then pour a glass of water over his leg. The pain didn't disappear, not fully, but it did temper, thanks to the dilution of the alcohol.

He let out a deep breath, then almost laughed at himself: the sound had been nearly orgasmic. He looked back at his leg. It was wetter than before, and most of the coagulate was washed from it, but otherwise it looked the same. Hooper grabbed the other glass of water, then hobbled away from the sink.

He made his way down the basement stairs, using his body to provide friction against the wall, so as not to tear the handrail from the wall. It seemed an eternity since his chase with Amy had reached its conclusion with the two of them tumbling down these steps, but it had been only a few hours earlier.

He came slowly off of the last step and looked at the cause of all of this. She was bound as she'd been when he left her, and he could tell that she was at least temporarily resigned to her imprisonment. The pole she was attached to had been painted red, and if she'd been trying to escape, there would have been paint shavings on the ground and on her hands.

Amy was either asleep or pretending to be so, and Hooper wanted to wake her so that he could discuss his injury with her, as well as the need to punish her for her attempted escape earlier that morning. He couldn't fault her for trying to get away, but it was still a behavior that needed to be broken from her, just like one would teach a child not to interrupt, or not to speak with a mouth full of food.

Hooper watched her lying there, beautiful in such a perfect way, and he decided that he'd let her sleep. He left the glass of water next to her, then made his way slowly up the stairs before shutting off the light.

It was still light outdoors, but Hooper ignored the window. He sat down heavily on the sofa, after turning on the TV. He had little use for the thing, especially right after one of his little hunting trips, but this was different. After all, Amy was *here*. He let his mind focus on the screen, and found a news station. There were boring stories about Iraq—who could possibly care?—and then, finally, *his* story. He beamed at the screen. They had found the body he'd left at the drive-in. Everything was coming together perfectly, except for getting shot. *They'll figure out time of death soon enough, and then they'll decide whoever claims to have shot me is full of shit.* It had been hard work, stealing a girl Amy's size, killing her, smashing her teeth with a hammer, then burning her and leaving her in a shallow grave, but all the effort had been worth it.

29

When Luke's mom finally came home, it was dark out and she was wasted. Luke had to help carry her to the couch. She fell asleep almost instantly, rolling over and then snoring. Ashley and Alisha had just watched him help her, moving off the couch only when it became obvious that was where Luke meant to put her. There was something depressing about having a mom who was too much of a wreck to even punish him, and Luke left her there to walk back to his room.

When Van Endel had come back to the room to tell him he was leaving with the Benchleys, Luke had been confused. Van Endel and that doctor lady had never even come back to talk to him. By the time he saw Mrs. Benchley and how furious she was, Luke had figured out most of it, all but the part about their finding Molly. *That's where they were wrong, though. The body they found couldn't have been Molly.* Mrs. Benchley had said that Molly had been dead for days, but that wasn't true, they had all seen her, and not one of them had questioned whether or not it was her. Why would they lie about something so terrible? A kidnapped kid, even a kidnapped teenager, was no laughing matter, and for Tim's and Scott's parents to think their kids capable of such a thing was almost as terrible as his own mother's condition.

Reviewing everything in his head, Luke figured it was likely that both Tim and Scott were going to be grounded for lengthy periods of time. Which left a whole separate issue: Molly. Mrs. Benchley had said that the body they found had been burned days earlier. How long would it take to check her fingerprints, or her teeth, if she was too badly burned, and realize they had the wrong girl? *Too long.* And really, any amount of time was too long. They knew three things. Molly wasn't dead, or at least she hadn't been this morning; the person who took her likely lived in the same area as they did, probably in Tim and Scott's neighborhood; and, most importantly, he had a gunshot wound in his right leg.

School was going to be a mess. They were headed for seventh grade and were likely to be branded as liars, a tag that would stick through the end of high school. After all, who would forget something like this? It was clear what needed to happen. They needed to find out where she'd been taken and see if she was still there. And either way, at that point, get the cops involved again, to save Molly, along with their reputations.

But how am I going to be able to do that on my own?

That was a tougher problem, tougher by a lot. It would be hard enough to find Molly and the man who took her with all three of them out and free, but with his friends on what he could only assume was lockdown, it seemed like it was going to be up to him.

The thought made Luke slump on his bed. He was just a regular kid, not some twelve-year-old genius detective. *This would be hard with all three of us, really hard, but I know I'm not smart enough to do it on my own.* Luke didn't even know where to start an investigation like that. Molly had just disappeared into the trees, and if the wounded man had left any sort of blood trail, the cops hadn't been able to find it. *Why did it have to rain?*

Then an idea began to form in his head. Not a brilliant one, but a small one, that could perhaps be added to with a little bit of luck. Luke figured they were due for some good luck—all three of them were, but especially him. He packed a bag with clothes, a small amount of food, and three Sprite caps. He left a note on the counter saying he would be back in a day or two, tops, and then waved at his zombified sisters as he left. They didn't even blink.

———

Scott had never felt so shell-shocked in his life. He had been ready to try to explain away some part of the story that got muddled because of Luke's shooting that guy, and maybe to get called out on it, but this was much worse than anything he could have anticipated. Carl had said that he was never going to be able to hang out with Luke or Tim ever again, and his mom had agreed with him—that was the ultimate betrayal. It would have been one thing for Carl to say something like that, and to then have his mom tell him that he was out of bounds, but she went right along with it. Why should Carl get to decide who he was friends with? *It's not like he's my real dad. Just because he married my mom doesn't give him the right to ruin my life.* It was all just so unfair, and no one was even willing to listen to them.

Scott couldn't even feel good about having seen Molly. The police and her parents thought she was dead, and soon she would be, if she wasn't already, he was sure of it. They had been given a chance to save her, and it had been taken away by adults who didn't listen when they needed to the most.

But what am I going to do about it? Nothing, that's what. He was going to sit in his room for the rest of the ruined summer, and that would be that. *Unless, when they do find the body, they realize that it must mean we were telling the truth!*

The realization of what that would mean sank in heavily. Molly would still be dead, and the best that could happen to him was that he might have some rights restored.

If he wasn't grounded, he could go look for the guy. They'd all seen him, and Scott knew he'd recognize him from what he'd seen of his face, as well as from what he felt sure would be a serious limp.

None of it mattered. He wasn't going anywhere. His mom had quit her job early so that she could be home with him—her choice, but his fault, according to her—and there was going to be no sneaking off to figure out what had happened. One thing did keep coming back to him, though it seemed almost impossible. What if he broke the house arrest but he and his friends figured out who had taken Molly? Could he get in trouble for that? Sure, they'd be mad at first, but they'd get over it, especially since they would have been wrong to ground him in the first place.

After imagining himself as the returning hero whose criminal past had been redeemed, Scott let the doubts fall out of his head like sand through his fingers: He was just one kid, Tim and Luke were grounded too, and they were the only people who knew that Molly was still in trouble. There was nothing that any of them could do about it, and there was nothing that was going to change that. He'd only just learned the phrase "catch-22," but that's what this was, and he was stuck in the middle of it. Scott lay in bed with his hands laced behind his head, wishing for the first time in his life that school would hurry up and get here already.

———

Tim walked to Becca's room after getting out of the shower and getting dressed. His dad had worked him like a dog in the baking sun, making him carry load after load of pea gravel into the backyard. Tim carried so much of it that he could actually see a difference from when they had started. When he tried to point that out to his dad, he was just told that he didn't need to talk to work. Tim discovered that his dad was right: after hearing that, he didn't want to talk either.

He needed to talk now, though. Now he needed to ask his sister some questions.

Tim knocked on her door, and a voice answered the knocking. "What?" said Becca.

"It's Tim. Can I come in?"

"Why? Want to lie to me or something?"

"No," said Tim. "I just wanted to talk to you. We're both grounded. It's not like you have anything better to do."

"What do you want to talk about?"

"I don't know. I'm just bored. Mom and Dad are super pissed, and I don't have anyone to talk to."

"Go away," said Becca from behind the door.

Tim opened his mouth to speak and then let it go. He walked back to his room and turned on the fan, then opened the window. It had cooled off, at least. Something on the windowsill caught his eye, and Tim slid the screen open. It was a Sprite cap, and a small piece of paper had been taped to it. The note said, "In the fort, next two nights."

Tim balled up the paper and stuffed it in the trash can by his desk, and put the Sprite cap in his pocket. Luke had a plan, and Tim didn't care what it was, he just wanted in. *Anything will be better than being stuck inside all summer, and it's not like I can get in any more trouble than I'm already in.*

Tim had been tired before the shower, and even more so after talking to Becca. Now, he still felt weary but was energized as well. He checked the clock radio: it was nine thirty. Tim set the alarm for 1:30, well past the time that his parents were normally asleep, and slid the clock under his pillow to muffle the sound. He shut off his lights and lay in bed, sure that he wouldn't sleep, but he was out in seconds.

30

Van Endel sat alone at the Shipwreck. It wasn't a cop bar, and that was what Van Endel liked about it. Most cop bars were full of bravado, with Irish and ancient police artifacts on the walls and cops drinking too hard for men who carried a gun as part of their day job. Van Endel had no use for shoptalk, especially not after a day like today. He was going to drink a beer or two, maybe have a scotch, then call it a night.

He'd been taking it pretty easy since waking up basically drunk the night that he'd first gotten the call about Molly. He felt guilty getting too out of sorts, had even considered the shame of getting called with a major lead and being too tight to act on it. To keep himself in check, that meant bar drinking. He could cut himself off a lot easier there, for some reason, and it was nice to be out of the house and not on the job at the same time.

The first few months since Lex had left him had been tough, but Van Endel was more worried about where he was headed these days. Lex was too far in the past to be an excuse for anything anymore, yet she still really was affecting his life. He didn't date, he didn't do anything. It felt like all he was doing was playing the miserable-cop cliché, always just managing his drinking and finances, never being anything more than the job.

She came into his life like a storm and left like one as well. They'd started dating in college, at Michigan State University, his plan for law enforcement, hers for veterinary medicine. Van Endel had graduated, but Lex hadn't, dropping out instead with what was to be the first of three failed pregnancies. They never talked about it later, but Van Endel knew in his soul that being a vet was something she had wanted to do, and was no longer something she still wanted for herself. Quitting for the baby that was never to be, and staying away from it for the babies that were never to be. Van Endel knew his long-suffering wife had given up on her dreams. What he didn't know until much later was that she blamed him.

Van Endel had worn a detective's shield for just six months when she left. It was the death knell to what Van Endel would have described as the best time of his life, had someone asked. They were doing good financially for once, even though Lex still wasn't working, and his goal had come to fruition. Being a detective was why he had started college, it was something he'd known he wanted to be since he'd first seen reruns of *87th Precinct* on TV, and later when reading books by the show's creator, Ed McBain. The show, and mostly the books, had made him see being a cop as something that some people were just built for, and he felt sure that he was one of them. Lex's leaving crippled that part of him.

Had she just left, that would have been one thing. He would have been bruised, but not broken. When she left, though, rage in her eyes and mouth, she'd told him how she really felt about her cop husband. She hated him for what he was. He was a pig, a phony, he was worthless to her. Van Endel hadn't known for sure that she was using cocaine behind his back until that moment, hadn't known that she was cheating on him. "You're such a shitty detective," she'd said, "that you didn't even know." The first of many confessions. She'd left that night, picked up by a sheepish man ten years her junior. Van Endel had left, and when he returned, the house was empty. He never even filed a police report for the stolen goods, just slowly and cheaply rebuilt his home, and who he was. Neither had turned out too well.

Van Endel finished the beer and stood, not feeling better, but feeling grounded. Molly Peterson was dead, and that was that. Now it was his job to find out who, and maybe even why, though usually the latter was nothing worth knowing. Van Endel slapped a ten-dollar bill on the bar, waved to the barkeep, and walked out.

31

The sound of the alarm woke Tim slowly, but once he realized what it was, he turned it off quickly. His heart was thumping in his chest as he slid out of bed. He was trying to be as quiet as possible, but every noise felt like the gunshot in the fort all over again. *Thank God I sleep with the door closed.* He got dressed in the clothes he'd helped his dad with the patio in—the last thing he needed was for one of his parents to notice extra laundry—walked to the window, and slid it the rest of the way open. He pushed in the buttons to raise the screen up, and it squeaked slightly as he moved it out of the way. Wincing at the squeak, Tim slid himself out of the window, then dropped silently into the bark around the landscaping. He gave a last look at the house, still not sure if this was a good decision, and took off running, headed straight for the path to the forest.

The grass made his feet wet through his sneakers, but Tim didn't care. The lights from some of the other houses gave off threatening beams of illumination that he avoided, and within just a few minutes he was in the darkness of the forest. Fumbling with the flashlight he'd stuck in his pocket and then turning it on, he began to run to the fort, no longer worried about noise or anything else. He just wanted to see his friends. Most of all, he was anxious to hear if Luke had come up with any other plans.

By the time he got to the ladder he was panting, but a glint from the forest floor made him smile. When he ran the flashlight over the spot, he saw two caps, Coke and Sprite. Tim dropped the Budweiser cap next to them, stuck the flashlight in his mouth, and began to climb.

When he got to the top and pulled himself into the fort, he felt his friends' hands pull him over the hole in the floor. He brushed himself off and then sat heavily by the window they'd been shooting from. It sure didn't feel like it had been less than a day since they'd been here, but that was the reality of it.

When he looked at his friends he saw smiles, and he didn't know if he'd ever been happier to see anyone in his whole life. "Think you're going to get caught?" Scott asked, and Tim smiled even wider. "No, but you probably are." All three of them erupted into tired giggles at that, and, not for the first time, Tim wondered at the logic in banning a kid from his best friends in the world.

"All right, all right," said Luke. "That's enough screwing around. We need to figure out a plan."

"To catch the guy?" Tim asked. "That's sort of what I figured we have to do to clear our names."

Luke and Scott exchanged a glance. "That's what we think too," said Scott. "It's our only option."

"So we all agree," said Luke, a touch of annoyance in his voice. "Great. But how are we going to do it?"

Tim thought about that. He hadn't really considered the middle step, he had just figured they'd find the guy who had kidnapped Molly, thus saving both her and the currently doomed summer. Nothing in his life had ever prepared him for how to find a kidnapper, not even a wounded one.

"Since neither of you is saying anything," said Luke, "I guess it will come down to me to figure this out. We were the last people to see Molly, right?" Tim and Scott nodded, and Luke continued.

"Here's the question, though. Besides us and the guy who took her, who else has seen her recently?" Tim and Scott just stared at Luke, waiting for an answer. Luke scowled and said, "Fine, I'll just figure the whole thing out for you guys. Becca saw her, Becca and all of her friends. And they all saw who she was with when she disappeared."

"That won't help," said Tim, a little forlornly. "Becca already told the cops everything, and they still can't find the guy."

Luke shook his head, and Tim wondered what else he'd missed. "Becca was with your folks when she talked to the cops, right?" Tim nodded, and Luke continued. "While she was already in trouble for how she was dressed—you told us that too. So here's the thing: What else were she and her friends doing that would have gotten her in even more trouble?"

"You mean like drugs or something, right?" Scott asked. "Because if it was something like that, no way was Becca going to rat herself out, especially if she'd already decided in her mind that Molly was perfectly safe."

Tim nodded. "It's true. Becca would lie about just about anything to keep from getting in trouble. It's just how she is. There's still a problem, though. How am I supposed to get her to tell me the truth?"

"You'll have to figure that part out on your own," said Luke. "You know your sister way better than we do. Plus we're not allowed in your house. What you need to find out, though, is who they were with, not just at the end, but all night. Who they were with, everywhere they went, everything. For all we know, one of them got some older guy to buy them cigarettes and he just followed them until he got the chance to get to Molly. The possibilities are pretty much endless. It's possible they never even went to the movies at all."

Tim was flabbergasted. Was Becca really capable of lying that well, to be able to fool both her parents and the police? He thought it was possible, but not very likely. Besides, what would be her motivation for lying in the first place? She knew one of her friends was in trouble; why try and hide information that could help the investigation from the police? There was only one explanation for any of that, and it could be only if they were doing something that would get her into huge trouble. Tim didn't know what that could be, or how to extract the information from her, but he knew he better come up with something fast.

"So here's the plan," said Luke. "Tim, you're going to talk to Becca and get the truth out of her. Do whatever it takes to get her to level with you, and make sure she tells you everything."

"Are we going to tell the cops?" Scott asked.

"No way in hell," said Luke. "That Van Endel guy might be smart, but he wouldn't believe a word out of our mouths, at least not until they figure out the body they found behind the drive-in isn't really Molly's. After that, he might even call us back in, but I don't think waiting is exactly in Molly's best interest."

"All right," said Tim. "I'll make Bacon an offer she can't refuse."

"Perfect," said Luke. "I'm going to stay in the fort until Saturday, minimum, so I can watch that trail that we saw them walk down. I don't think they'll come back, but you never know. Plus, if I'm here all the time and one of you guys needs to run away—like if you get busted for sneaking out—we'll have an easy meeting place to start from."

"Wait," said Scott. "Are you not in trouble? Because Tim and I are in, like, all the trouble, and you get to stay out of the house for a few days?"

"It's not quite like that," said Luke darkly. "I'm kind of already running away. My mom came home super drunk last night, and I decided the punishment she would give me when she was hungover from that wasn't worth sticking around for."

"Aren't you worried she'll come looking for you?"

"Guys, I know this sounds weird, and probably even a bit dramatic, but except for the stuff I do around the house to help out, my mom would rather not have me there at all. I know that you both come from normal families and that might sound crazy, but it's true. This way will be easier, and hopefully there will be nothing for me to even be in trouble over by the time we're done."

"Anything else?" Tim asked.

"Nope. You both have normal days, and we'll meet back here at the same time tomorrow night."

32

The night felt like it had been a dream, when Tim woke, exhausted, to his mother pounding on his bedroom door. He called, "I'm up, Mom," before even looking at the clock. When he did, he saw it was seven in the morning.

He slid out of bed, and the sight of himself in his mirror stopped him. It hadn't been a dream. He really had snuck out, made a plan with his friends, and, just as stealthily, snuck back into the house unnoticed. He threw on new clothes and walked to the kitchen, making sure not to smile as he entered.

His mom was frying bacon and cracking eggs for scrambling, while his dad was reading at the table. Becca was nowhere to be found, so Tim assumed she was sulking in her room.

Tim walked to the table and sat down. "Ready to get to work, Dad?"

His dad eyed him over the book. "I'm ready to watch you work. I'm taking a day off. You might want to get yourself some breakfast. It's a long time until lunch."

"But Mom—"

"Your mother is making a hot breakfast for herself and for me. You may have cereal, and there are some bananas that aren't quite bad yet."

Tim stood and walked back to get his cereal. They were really taking this seriously! He smiled but kept it on the inside. There was no reason for them to see it, or to risk their thinking he might be up to something. He was winning, no matter how hard they thought they were punishing him. He had snuck out and back in successfully, and seen the two people they had barred him from ever seeing again. *They're going to feel terrible when they find out I didn't lie, and I'm never going to accept an apology for it.* That thought did make Tim smile, and he banished the dangerous expression from his face as he began to pour milk over the cereal.

Work, as Tim knew it would be, was hard. He spent the morning suffering with loads of heavy rock, while his father sat in a chair, drinking a glass of ice water. The worst part was the no talking. His father was a super-good friend, and as bad as it was being banished from his other friends, it was almost worse having this one be so unfriendly.

As morning faded slowly to afternoon and the pile of rock got smaller, Tim thought of Becca, and how in the world he was going to get his sister to listen to him long enough to even start a conversation. And that was the easy part! Staring at the blade of the transfer shovel, Tim knew that if he was going to escape this project, he was going to need to get his sister to hate him a lot less than normal.

Good luck with that.

———

Scott was folding laundry. His mom had said that he needed to keep himself busy all day, or she was going to come up with something far worse than anything he could possibly conceive of to do.

The mood in the house had gone from wonderful, with the news of Carl's new position and raise at work, to morose sadness. Scott's mom was upset all the time, and even Carl looked down, as if he had finally started to come around on the idea of raising another man's son but was now starting to reevaluate things. Scott felt bad for reasons he didn't understand. Sure, he had stolen the gun and would have lied to the police, but all the stuff he was actually in trouble for lying about was true. His mom called down to him, interrupting the folding.

"Carl just called. When he gets home from work, you two are going to work on the Olds."

Scott smacked the palm of his hand into his forehead. "All right." He paused, trying to think of a way to get out of being alone with Carl. "Doesn't Hooper usually help Carl out with that stuff? It's not like I know anything. I'll probably just piss him off even more than he already is."

"I'm sure you'll do fine. As for Hooper, Carl says he's under the weather. Probably just being lazy, if you ask me. But none of that matters. You need to be done with whatever task you're on when Carl gets home, got it?"

Scott sighed loudly, but not loudly enough for her to hear upstairs. "Yes, Mom. I got it." It was only 2:10. *Today is going to last forever.*

When Carl came home, Scott went out to meet him. "It's going to be a minute," said Carl. "I need to get out of these clothes. I'm not going to ruin work shit working on that goddamn wrecker."

Scott nodded, watching as Carl walked inside. He began to pull plastic toolboxes from carefully organized shelves, the kind that were carefully placed and could be placed back just as carefully. Scott laid the wrench boxes on the floor of the garage and had one left in his hand when the door from the house slammed shut. It was very loud, and very convincing that things were not going to go well. But Carl's smile changed things.

"Hey, liar," said Carl. "How's it feel to be a piece of crap?"

"Not good," said Scott, grimacing. "Not good at all."

"Yeah, I figured you'd be pretty down. That's why I bought you some free time outside. You can watch and help a little bit if you want, but I can do most of the heavy lifting. You got my wrenches?"

"Sure, right here," said Scott, handing the heavy toolbox to Carl. "Why are you being nice to me?"

Scott regretted the words the instant they came out of his mouth, and his face flushed. Surprisingly, though, Carl didn't look mad. In fact, he looked like he was remembering an old joke with some fondness. "Before I say anything," he said, "I want you to know that I'll deny telling you any of this. Got it?" Scott nodded. "OK. First off, I believe that you and your buddies were telling the truth."

"You do?" Scott asked, incredulous. "If you believe us, then why did you punish me?"

Carl shrugged. "Your mom knew what she wanted to happen, and I didn't see any way of convincing her otherwise without getting my tail stuck in a crack next to yours. There are a lot of delicate things to consider here, but one of them is that as much as she wanted a man influencing your life, she also still wants to be the one making the majority of the decisions regarding you. She told me what she wanted to happen after talking to Tim's mom, and I went along for the ride, not that I had much of a choice. I believe your little story, or at least most of it."

"How do you mean?"

"Who knows if you actually saw Molly in the woods? The cops seem pretty convinced that they found her body by the drive-in, and they're usually right about that sort of thing."

"But if we saw someone else—"

"Then maybe someone else was taken. Guys who do this kind of thing usually like the same sort of things every time, so if he took Molly, then he might have taken another girl who looked like Molly. Or you could have really seen her. It's pretty tough to say until they run her fingerprints or do a dental impression."

"What will happen then?"

"Well, if it turns out not to be her, I imagine you'll end up with a reduced sentence. Not to mention, the police will look pretty stupid for not acting on a live lead. Of course, the real shame would be for Molly. If you guys did see her, and at least a glimpse of the guy who took her, she might have had a chance of being rescued, and now that chance is gone." Carl opened the hood of the Oldsmobile and sighed. "Where do we even start?"

—

While Tim slaved away and Scott did the same, only more willingly, Luke sat alone with his thoughts in the fort. It wasn't the most entertaining thing, just staring into the woods, but it was sort of relaxing, and it beat the hell out of being home with his hungover mom and terrible sisters.

He had seen two people in the woods that afternoon, two boys a couple of years older than he, smoking cigarettes and laughing, passing a few hundred feet from the fort without noticing it. Luke had enjoyed watching them as a hunter, even though they were not prey. There was something to be said for going unnoticed. It was a thrill, even though he was doing nothing more than sitting in a wooden box.

Luke leaned back against one of the walls. A quick nap wouldn't hurt anything. He let impossible thoughts take him to slumber. A clean trailer, a sober mother, the heartfelt apology from Van Endel. It was going to be good.

He slept for a couple of hours, as the calculator watch told him when he finally came to around six o'clock. Had Luke been awake, he might have seen that there was another person in the woods that day, a man carrying binoculars and walking with a limp. Unlike Luke, that man was hunting and was quite sure that he had found out exactly where his quarry had been roosting.

33

Hooper woke on the couch. Looking back and forth between the clock on the wall and the light coming through the blinds, he finally worked out that he had slept in until nearly three in the afternoon.

He stood slowly, testing his weak leg, and was shocked to see that it was feeling a little better than the day before. He hobbled his way to the bathroom, then sat on the toilet like an invalid to urinate. When he was done he turned on the shower and stripped off his underwear. The water felt nice but didn't bring the clarity he was used to. His leg was far too distracting, the water on it felt like someone running broken glass across his skin. Giving up after just a few short and decidedly unsatisfying minutes, Hooper dried off and opened the medicine cabinet. He poured three aspirin into his mouth from the bottle and chewed them into a bitter powder, then swallowed. It was time to check on Amy.

He made toast and carried it with him to the steps, then made his way down them, careful not to spill the bread. She was awake, he saw when he reached the bottom, with her back to the pole. He felt cruel setting the plate next to her. She was gagged and bound, after all, and had to be starving, but there was one more thing to be done before she could eat. He tried to avoid her eyes as he said, "I'll be right back," before slowly making his way back up the stairs. Once at the top, he went to the garage to get the chain and locks from his car, and then headed back downstairs.

When he was finally in the basement again, he undid one of Amy's arms and then the other, then refastened them in front of her. He half expected her to fight, and took her passivity as a good sign. Everyone has a breaking point, and hopefully she was getting closer to hers, perhaps was even there already. He wound the chain around the pole five times, then locked two links together, so that it made a very solid five-foot-long leash. Amy would be able to stand, but barely. He took the other end of the chain, looped the lock through it, and attached it to the metal ring on the collar around her neck.

"I'm going to take your gag off now," said Hooper. "And if you scream, no one is going to hear you, but you will be punished. I already owe you a lashing for yesterday, so think it through." He gently loosened the straps on the back of the gag, and she fell upon the water he'd cruelly left her the night before. In his injured state, he hadn't realized the glass would just provide torment, as she would have been unable to drink it. She drank greedily at first, and then seemed to consider the idea that she should make it last. She set the cup down half empty, then began to eat the dry toast.

"This will be our arrangement for a few days," said Hooper. "If you keep up the good behavior, I'll bring you more to eat than just bread and water." He looked at the slowly drying spot on the floor where she had pissed, and grabbed an empty five-gallon bucket from under the steps. "You can use this as a toilet—again, at least until I know I can trust you."

"Does your leg hurt?" Amy asked him in a timid, kind-sounding voice.

"It does," he said. "I was hurt in the war, by shrapnel, and this feels a little bit like that," he said, then chuckled. "Maybe a little worse. I was a much younger man then, and they had me on painkillers almost immediately. Walking is easier than I expected it to be, so that's a blessing."

"What are you going to do with me? If you let me go, I won't tell anyone what's happened, and I don't even know where I am, not really." She was smiling at Hooper, but unlike when she kindly asked after his injury, this was not a smile to be nice. She was trying to manipulate him. He walked behind her. She didn't turn to follow him, though he was sure she must have wanted to. Hooper grabbed the chain with both hands and yanked, jerking her back into the pole and making Amy grunt with pain. He dropped the chain and walked to where she could see him again. She was crying, looking at the floor while sobs wracked her body. *It's not my fault that I need to discipline her. She tried to run away, that's how this whole mess started, and if I'm not stern enough, problems like that will persist.*

Hooper knelt in front of her, then tenderly lifted her head by the chin. "You need to understand some things, Amy. You belong to me now. There is no going back to what you had before. This is your life now. The sooner you accept that, the better for both of us." He smiled, and she smiled back, but he knew it was forced. Her eyes were red and puffy, her face bruised slightly from the fall down the steps, he assumed. "Do what you're told, and things will get better, do you understand?"

She nodded and said quietly, "Yes."

"Good. Now I'm going to go back upstairs, so give me your hands and then sit against the pole." She did as instructed, and as a reward, he cuffed them behind her, but not around the pole. She was plenty well secured to it without that, anyway. Next, he replaced the ball gag in her mouth and then tightened the straps. When she looked at him now, all defiance, all hope even, was gone from her face. Hooper smiled at her and then shuffled up the steps, returning her to darkness and locking the door behind him.

The business with Amy taken care of, Hooper walked to his room. He'd decided that there was something else that needed doing, regardless of his injured state. He went to his closet and pulled out a set of olive drab fatigues, pants, and a long-sleeved shirt. He put the pants on slowly, then pulled on and buttoned the shirt, before taking a matching flat-brimmed hat down from the top of the closet and mashing it onto his head. If someone saw him, he might think Hooper was being a little nutty, but if pressed on the matter, Hooper planned to ask if that guy could still fit into his clothes from twenty years ago. His neighbors were good folks; they'd just think he was screwing around. He tucked the small revolver into a pocket and headed for the sliding door.

It was odd being in the backyard again. The last time, leading Amy with the gun, still seemed surreal. He walked to the gate, opened it, and walked into the woods. Someone had been hunting him yesterday, and he wanted to know who. There was a bullet in his calf, and Hooper deserved to know who had put it there. He backtracked his steps as well as he could remember, following the broken path of popples back to where he'd been shot. There was no blood to show him where it had happened, the rain would have seen to that, but somehow Hooper just knew when he was in the spot.

The moment had been frozen into his memory, and he could picture the day before with astonishing clarity. This was where he'd forced Amy into the thick trees, his calf burning with pain. Turning slowly, he oriented himself both to where he had been and to where his back would have been facing. Hooper almost jumped when he saw the fort through the trees. *How did I not see it before?* The stress of the day must have dulled his normally excellent situational awareness.

The fort was made of weathered lumber and was attached to three trees, one much larger than the others. On the side closest to him, Hooper could see a window cut into a plywood wall. It made him nervous. That was undoubtedly where the shot had come from.

He advanced on the fort as though approaching an enemy emplacement, for that was just what it was. Carl had mentioned something about helping his son with a fort back in the woods, Hooper recalled as he crept up on it. This was probably the same one. *And I bet Carl's fucking kid was one of the ones who shot me.* The thought set off a burst of black rage in his head, tempered only slightly by relief that the boy clearly hadn't recognized him.

When he reached the fort, Hooper peered up at its floor and listened. Hearing nothing, he put the foot of his good leg on the bottom rung of one of the ladders leading up to the fort and began to climb. When he put weight onto his injured leg, though, his body shut down, his calf betraying him, and Hooper fell a few feet to the forest floor, landing on his ass.

He was OK, but his dignity had taken a beating. It was for the best, he decided as he brushed himself off, feeling ridiculous in the old, musty-smelling clothes. He couldn't hear the kids up there, but for all he knew, they could be there, armed and waiting on him. Though if they were holed up there as silently as this and were still armed with what he assumed was something stolen from Carl's ridiculous gun collection—a .22, judging from the hole in his calf—they would have heard his tumble from the ladder and already taken a shot at him. Still, as he walked away from the fort the same way he'd come, he was cautious, even more nervous with his back facing the maw of the window. He might not see to them today, but he would teach those kids respect, and soon.

34

Van Endel was sitting at his desk, contemplating another cup of coffee, when the phone rang. "Van Endel," he said. There was a moment of silence, then a clicking sound, and Tracy was on the line.

"What's shaking, Mr. Detective?"

"Nothing, Tracy," said Van Endel, and he meant it. Since the body had been found, he hadn't been able to put his hands on one shred of evidence. It was beyond frustrating, but Tracy calling could mean that there had been a breakthrough at the coroner's office. "What do you have for me?"

"A little bit of interesting news—maybe good; not my call— and a big old chunk of frustrating news. You got a preference?"

"I'll take frustrating."

"I've got nothing on dental so far," said Tracy. "Big fat zilcho, and I don't see that changing."

"So you still can't say with any certainty that this actually is Molly?"

"Nope, sure can't. I took a bunch of pictures to share with my old professor. He has some contacts in New York, said he can see if they can help. I'm good, but these teeth are something else. If the guy was deliberately trying to disguise who she was, he couldn't have done a better job of it. I'm guessing that's exactly what his goal was. I've heard of Mob guys doing stuff like that, burying Jimmy Hoffa with no head, hands, or feet, that sort of thing. Whoever did this knew that fire would destroy her fingerprints and footprints, and that hammer he used, I'm damn sure on that, plain old claw hammer, you can tell by the impre—"

"I'll take your word for it, Tracy."

"All right, whatever," Tracy said, sounding a little miffed that Van Endel didn't share his enthusiasm for the bloody nuts and bolts of his trade. "Anyways, I got the teeth thing headed out of state, so we'll see what those guys have to say.

"Now the other thing, though. The interesting one. She had a leather wallet in a back pocket, it was basically seared into her. At first I thought it was just more skin. You want to guess what was in there?" The line was silent for a minute, and Tracy sighed. "Won't even try. You just know you can't get it right, so you won't even play."

"Tracy."

"All right, all right. Latex residue, along with some ruined foil. I got them under the microscope, confirmed on both."

"Condoms."

"My man gets the assist, anyway," said Tracy. "So here's how I see it. You either accept that Molly might have been planning on having a little safe fun, and things got out of hand, or that something else is going on."

"Like what?"

"Shit, I don't know," said Tracy. "You're the detective, I'm the lab rat. I can tell you what, where, and when it was done to her. You're the one who figures out the who and why. One thing, though: I can't think of any reason for anyone to kill Molly Peterson and go to all this effort to keep her identity a secret, can you?"

"No," admitted Van Endel. "There has to be some explanation, though. You're right: disguising the body like this took time, and he ran a hell of a risk burning it like he did, too. I can't see why anyone would do it just to do it."

"Is the mom clean?"

"Stick to the what, where, and when, Tracy. That was one of the first things I looked into. Mom works a steady job, drinks a little, doesn't date."

"So no Mob ties or gambling debts?"

"Let me know what you hear on the teeth, all right?" Van Endel hung up the phone, frowning at nothing, and looking at and through his desk. *There has to be a reason.* The problem was that one of the truths he'd learned as a detective was that there didn't have to be a good reason. Husbands beating wives to death for the hell of it, kids putting shotguns in their mouths because of heavy-metal songs, moms drowning infants in shallow bathtubs. Bad things happened often and never needed to schedule an appointment before they dropped on in.

And still he kept grinding at the why. Could the guy—it had to be a guy, anything else was impossible to Van Endel—who did it have been so ashamed by what he'd done that he'd needed to try his hardest to destroy the evidence? Van Endel didn't believe it. There had to be more to why someone would murder a teenage girl and then destroy the corpse beyond recognition.

35

Tim walked quietly down the hall toward Becca's room. He wasn't sure what the rules were concerning him and his sister fraternizing during their respective groundings, but he figured the less his folks knew at this point, the better. He tapped twice on the door, waited for a response, and then tapped twice again. "What?" Becca called from inside the room. "I'm just in here reading."

"It's Tim. Can I come in?"

"Why?"

"I need to ask you something."

"You're lucky I'm bored."

"So I can come in?"

"Yes, hurry up."

He'd rarely seen the inside of his sister's room in the past few years, and he took in the sights the same way a traveler voyaging to forbidden lands would. The walls were covered in posters for bands like Mötley Crüe and Guns N' Roses, and all the people on the posters looked as though they were going insane. Men dressed like women, with big, teased-out, dyed hair. They wore very little clothing—what there was was mostly leather and spiky—and were covered in tattoos. As Tim lived in a household sans MTV, it was a small culture shock.

"Stop staring at everything," Becca said from atop her covers. "What do you want?"

"I want to ask you some questions about what happened the night Molly got taken."

"Nope," said Becca, her eyes returning to the hardcover book she was reading. "I already told Mom, Dad, and the cops everything that happened. Not that it's any of your business, and not that anything I could tell you is going to help you out of the hole you've lied yourself into. Trust me, if you go to Mom with any more stories, you're just going to get in more trouble." She turned a page in her book violently. "If that's even possible."

"Maybe I can get in more trouble, maybe I can't," said Tim. "But I do know one thing. You could get in way more trouble if I tell Mom what you were really doing."

"I was at the movies, duh. Best of luck. Don't let the door hit your ass on the way out."

Tim gave her a look that she met and matched. He knew that he needed to get her attention, and do it fast, or he was never going to hear the truth. "Aren't you even worried about Molly?"

She threw herself upright against the headboard, the book closed, forgotten on her lap. "That's a shitty thing to ask me, you little turd. Of course I'm worried about Molly. Not that it's doing any good. The cops think she's dead."

"I don't think you are," said Tim, treading in shark-infested water. "In fact, I think you and your friends are sort of hoping maybe she won't come back, and then none of you will get busted for what really happened."

"You shut up. You can't just barge in here saying all this awful shit. My friend got kidnapped, and you and your stupid friends got jealous and made up some dumb lie that you immediately got caught telling, and now you want to bring me down to your level."

Tim took a deep breath. It was time to go for the kill. Becca was teed up for it. "You aren't even considering one thing," he said in a measured tone. "My friends are telling the truth, and so am I. I'm telling you, we saw Molly with a dark-haired guy in the woods. He had a gun to her back. A black gun, and Molly was scared out of her mind."

Becca grimaced slightly at that. It was barely there, but Tim saw it.

"Well, good job, Becca. You and all your friends lied, and now one of your best friends is going to die. That detective might think he caught the real liar, but he's wrong. You haven't told anyone the truth."

"Shut up, would you?" Her face was paling by the second, and her eyes were sparkling with greasy-looking tears. "Just shut up!"

"You need to tell the truth, Becca. She'll die if you don't."

"I *can't*," she said, backhanding the tears from her eyes and glaring at him. "I *can't*. It's terrible...we'd be in so much trouble. Mom and Dad would, like, I don't know, disown me, or send me off somewhere."

"You guys weren't at the movies at all, were you?"

Becca shook her head back and forth, tears streaming down her face. Tim knew that now that she was started she'd tell him the whole thing, she'd be desperate to blurt out every sordid detail of what had really happened Monday night. For better or for worse, Tim was going to get the truth.

"They threatened me, said that if I told anyone, I was done at the high school. If I was lucky they'd just kick my ass, or maybe even something worse would happen."

"Why did they not want Molly found?"

"Tim, you don't get it," said Becca, exasperated with him. "That happened before we went out. All the threats, the *don't tell anyone, ever*—all that happened before Molly was gone, before we were even there."

"What are you talking about? What were you doing?"

Becca adjusted herself on the bed, managing to look both comfortable and miserable at the same time. "Go check the door," she said. "Make sure Mom's not out there, and if she's not, shut it quietly." Tim did, and when he came back, he sat at the foot of the bed. "The older guys called it fishing. A bunch of girls dress up really skanky, and then they drive us down to South Division Street, the bad part. The girls get dropped off, and the guys go to a couple of motel rooms, except for a couple of them, who stay in the alley to protect us."

"But what were you doing?"

"We were pretending to be hookers," said Becca matter-of-factly. "And when a guy picked one of us up, we'd tell him to go to the motel because we have a room. The customer or whatever comes up with the girl, and once he's in the room, a bunch of the guys jump him and take all of his money. He can't call the cops because he was breaking the law, and we all split the money up.

"I did it, like, once. My shirt got ripped when the guy I brought up grabbed me. He was super pissed and really scary. Anyways, Molly got picked up and never showed up. Then we heard that cops were coming on the police scanner that Tyler brought, and we all had to leave. I figured she just got to the motel after we had to leave and got arrested, or had to do, well, what the guy wanted."

"Becca, what *is* a hooker, exactly?"

"Jesus," she said. "You're such a baby. It's someone who has sex for money. That's how we knew all the guys would have cash. They were going shopping, just not for groceries."

Tim let it all sink in. He understood most of it but didn't want to feel stupid by asking too many questions. "So this guy could be anyone?"

"Yep," said Becca. "And whether that's Molly by the drive-in or not, there's no way she's still OK."

"Unless we can find who took her," Tim said. "It's someone from this neighborhood. You guys might have been downtown, but he came back here. You know how I can prove it? When we saw his gun, Luke shot him in the leg with Scott's stepdad's rifle."

Becca snapped to attention. "You really did see them—like, for real?"

"That's what I've been saying. Why the hell would we make it up? Not only did we see them, we hurt him. Now we just need to find out who he is."

They were both quiet for a long minute, staring at each other without really seeing each other. Then Becca said, "Well, it's been raining a lot. Everybody's lawn is going to grow a ton. If he really did got shot in the leg, there's no way he's mowing his lawn."

Tim's mouth dropped open, and then a banging on the door made them both jump. "Tim, get out of your sister's room and go pick up everything outside," said their dad. "Storm's coming."

"One more thing," said Tim, quietly. "You said there were people watching to make sure you guys were safe, right?" She nodded. "You need to see if they can tell you the type of car Molly got into. We know he lives around here."

"I'll try, but I'm grounded from the phone."

"Just try," pleaded Tim. He stood and waved to his sister, smiling sadly. She gave the same look back, because Molly really was in trouble, and Becca had to know that it was her and her friends' fault.

36

The wild beeping of Scott's watch alarm shocked him awake and sent him scrambling to silence it. His mom and Carl were just across the hall but, impossibly, didn't stir. Heart hammering, he eased out of bed, pulled on dirty clothes as Tim had suggested, removed his window screen, and slid to the earth, thankful that he didn't have a second-floor bedroom.

The air was cooler than it had been the night before, and Scott was briefly sorry he hadn't brought a sweatshirt with him. He reached the fort in no time, though. He threw his Coke cap down, noticing that tonight he was the third man to the party. He scrambled up the ladder and threw himself over the threshold at the top to find his friends grinning and waiting for him. "Glad you could make it, slowpoke," Tim teased, and Scott faked a punch at him before sitting. "Any news?"

"Nothing on my end," said Luke. "I sat in the fort all day and didn't see anything."

"I talked to my sister," Tim said, and then began to relay what she'd told him. The fake-prostitution trick, the way Molly had really been taken, the tip about looking for little signs in the suburban neighborhood, like unkempt lawns, and finally, the idea to have her try to figure out the make and model of the car the man who took Molly had been driving. He went through it breathlessly, racing to relay the information.

"OK, that's some really messed-up shit," said Luke. "Like really messed up. You guys are under house arrest and I had to run away from home for a little bit, but your sister and her friends have gotten away with robbing people? It's no wonder that Van Endel dude didn't believe us. I'll bet he knew they were lying to him too." Luke shook his head and frowned. "That's messed up, like, big-time."

"I know," said Tim. "It is messed up, but at least we know the truth now. We know more than anyone else about what's happening, and if anyone is going to save Molly, it's going to be us."

"Are you sure we can't just go to the police?" Scott asked. "I know they don't believe us, but it seems like it would be worth a try. After all, we're grounded. How are we supposed to go looking for this guy?"

"That's just it," Tim said. "We're grounded. So how are we supposed to have figured out all this stuff we're going to tell the police? Our folks'll send us to military school or something if they find out what we've been up to."

Scott rolled his eyes at the military-school part, but he had to admit Tim had a point. "I suppose," he said. "But that lawn thing—it's neat and all, but we just shot that guy. It will be two weeks, minimum, before we'll be able to notice who isn't mowing their lawn. For all we know, he could even be better by then." He shook his head. "I just don't see this plan working, unless your sister can come through with more information on the car, and that doesn't seem very likely."

The three boys brooded in silence for a few minutes, until Tim broke the spell. "Look, we knew this was going to be hard. We can't get discouraged by that. We just need to do what we can and hope that it's enough." Scott and Luke were both nodding at that, and Luke said, "So what's the game plan for tomorrow?"

Tim said, "I'm going to find some way to distract my parents so that Becca can make a quick phone call."

"I can try and borrow a pistol from Carl's stash tomorrow," Scott said. "It won't be easy, and I'd really hate to be caught with it, but damn, we're going to need something. Hey, I forgot to tell you guys, Carl actually believes us."

"Seriously?" Luke asked. "Then why are you grounded?"

Scott grinned. "Because my mom is so gung ho about me being punished that Carl just kind of had to be like, 'Fuck it, she wants the kid punished, I'll punish him.' It put him in a pretty bad spot, and I actually felt bad for him. It still sucks, but at least one adult believes us. It's better than nothing."

"Yeah, I guess so," said Luke. "I'll just walk around and see if anything looks out of place, I guess. I'm going to need to go home soon too, though. My mom will clear her head out eventually and come looking for me, and if I'm not at either of your two houses, there's really only one place to go." He rapped twice on one of the walls. "Aside from the mosquitoes, it's been pretty nice staying up here. Better a few mosquito bites than hanging out with my sisters."

"So are we good, then?" Tim asked. "The sooner we're home, the less likely it is that we get caught."

The three boys stood, and Tim and Scott left by ladder, taking their bottle caps with them and leaving one lonely Sprite cap all by itself.

37

Hooper was alone. He was running through the jungle with his M16, and the VC were everywhere. Explosions were going off left and right, and all he could hear around him was the crackling of AK fire, along with Charlie screaming at him. Hooper didn't know where he was running, only that he was alone and that he was in the middle of a death trap. They'd fallen for one of the VC's favorite tricks: set up a patrol to look like it was lost, and when the good guys went after them, spring a trap of tiger pits and snipers. Hooper had been in a few ambushes before, but nothing like this.

It was almost impossible to believe he'd lived this long in the shit. He had no idea where the good guys were, or even if there were any left. He felt like he was behind enemy lines, but he had no idea who was bombing whom. Not that it was impossible for some general to have given wrong coordinates to some gunner or pilot, but there was an insane amount of shit going off. Hooper just wanted to be away from the killing, away from this hell on earth.

Somehow, in an instant that made zero sense, Hooper knew that a sniper was glassing him from behind, getting the reticules of his rifle lined up just right on Hooper's back, adjusting for windage and elevation, and readying to pull the trigger. Hooper heard the crack of the rifle over all of the other noise. It didn't make any sense, but above the screaming, AK fire, and explosions, the crack of the sniper's rifle was the sound of an angry but far-away God. Pain erupted in his right calf, dropping him and tearing a scream from Hooper's throat.

When Hooper woke up, it was the middle of the night and he was covered in a slick sheen of sweat. He ignored the clock; time didn't matter right now. His leg was killing him, and he wasn't going to be able to sleep, possibly ever again, until he got the damn metal out of his leg.

He'd been dreaming about Vietnam. It had been years since that had happened. Some guys let that fuck up their whole lives, but not Matt Hooper. His bad dreams had stopped when he'd started snatching and stabbing prostitutes, and they weren't going to come back, not ever. He cursed under his breath, then stood and walked to the bathroom.

He pissed, then opened the medicine cabinet, took out the aspirin, and ate six of them, washing the bitter powder down with water cupped in his hands from the sink. His leg had been feeling fine before he went to bed, but now it was more painful than ever. *Calm down, Hoop. You knew as soon as that happened that that bullet had to come out of there. You've just been lying to yourself about it.* Hooper tried grunting away the internal voice of reason, then accepted it. The bullet needed to come out, and there was only one person who could help him. Hooper left the bathroom, walked to the kitchen, then filled a pot with water and set it on the stove. He turned the burner all the way up and walked to the garage.

His fishing and camping stuff was all in the rafters, lying on an old door. Hooper's interest in the outdoors had faded years ago, so there was no need to make it more readily accessible. As he wrestled the folding ladder off of the wall, he regretted that decision more than almost any other that he'd ever made. When he finally had the ladder set up next to the Dodge, he rested and glared up at the rafters. There was going to be no way to do this without putting pressure on his injured leg. It was the only option. Hooper took a deep breath, released it, and began to climb.

Hooper discovered after the very first rung that he'd grossly underestimated the pain that would be involved in this business. He accepted that and went on with it anyway, grunting and squealing as he made his agonizing way to the rafters to retrieve the tackle box. With every step, his leg felt as though it were being worked over with a knife. The worst part was knowing that as bad as this was, the extraction was likely going to be far, far worse.

With his good leg on the fourth rung of the ladder, Hooper could just reach the bottom of the door. Sweat was pouring off of him in what felt like rivers, and his hands were slick with it. His whole body felt as though it had been dipped in oil. He struggled up two more steps, his body tense as a parachutist's static line, all but ready to rip open and fly apart. Hooper placed his left hand on the door, and then the right, pulling on it to take some of the strain off of his hurt leg. He rummaged blindly atop the door until he located the ancient tackle box with the very tips of his roaming fingers. He strained and scratched at it until he finally found enough purchase to inch it closer and closer. At last he reached the handle and dragged it to the edge.

Hooper set the box on top of the ladder and took a moment to rest and enjoy this minor triumph before setting to conquering the ladder in reverse. He managed to descend two rungs, but then his injured foot clipped a rung and he was airborne, the tackle box still firmly gripped in one hand, his other scrabbling futilely for a hold on the ladder. The moment didn't last long. Hooper went from flying to landing with a teeth-rattling crash on the hood of the Dodge, the tackle box's contents exploding across the garage.

The world flashed from black, to black and white, to black again. When Hooper opened his eyes, he was lying on his back on the hood of the Dodge, his leg, back, and head screaming. He pulled himself to a sitting position and then slid from the car and collapsed on all fours onto the garage floor.

He shook his head once to clear it, then tried again. It wasn't working.

The last memories he'd had were of Vietnam and being shot, but he was in his garage. Even through the pain, Hooper knew that he had not really just been in the jungle. *You're in your garage,* he told himself. *You were getting your fishing stuff down from the rafters. Why?* The bullet's strike flashed back to him, but why had he been shot if he really hadn't been in Vietnam?

Amy.

The thought of her brought it all back, and Hooper slowly began gathering his wits, along with the scattered supplies from the tackle box. He kept a neat garage, thankfully, but it still took him a long time to gather the things he needed. When he'd finally located the two small forceps he used to tie flies, he stood, using the car for support. He groaned when he saw the hood. The damage may have been only cosmetic, in the form of one large, man-shaped dent, but it would need to be fixed. There was no way someone like Carl could see the car in this condition and not ask him what in the hell had happened to it. Hooper shook his aching head, thinking about the repair bill—engine work was something he could do, but body work wasn't—then headed into the house.

He went to the bedroom first and took the small revolver from the nightstand before limping to the kitchen, where he found the pot of water boiling over. He dropped the forceps into the water and then reduced the heat. After scrounging through the knife drawer, he selected a paring knife with a three-inch blade and held its tip in the water for a few minutes. Then he grabbed a plate and a pair of tongs and used the tongs to retrieve the forceps, which he set on the plate with the knife. Finally, he shut off the stove and dragged his afflicted leg toward the basement, the plate and steaming makeshift instruments in one hand, the bottle of

Everclear in the other, and with the pistol tucked into the waist-band of his briefs.

He slid down the steps in the way he was becoming accustomed to, with his body pressed against the wall to take as much weight as possible off of his leg. He made the bottom without dropping the plate or the bottle, though he could feel his underwear was in dire need of hiking up. The pistol was slipping from his waistband, and with his hands full, Hooper was unable to retrieve it as it slowly slid next to and then under his dick, the weight of it tugging down his shorts a precarious couple of inches.

Amy was just starting to come to, but her eyes widened when he set the plate down and she saw what was on it. "Calm down," said Hooper. "That shit ain't for you." He reconsidered and said, "At least, not in the way you might be thinking."

He set the Everclear next to the plate, both of them just out of what he figured would be her reach, then walked behind her. Seeing Amy normally made him hot, but today sex was the furthest thing from his mind. His cock felt small and useless next to the cold steel of the revolver, and Hooper removed the gun and held it next to his leg, happy to have it out of his shorts.

Hooper set the pistol on the ground and removed her handcuffs, noting the red stripes that were banding both of her wrists from the weight of her bonds. When he circled her again, she was sitting patiently like a good girl with her hands in her lap, so he bent down to loosen the straps, keeping the ball gag in her mouth. "Same rules as last time, Amy," he said, then plucked the gag from her lips.

"I need some water," she rasped. "Please, can I please have some water?"

"When we're done," said Hooper. "You got to help me first, though." He pointed at his leg but didn't look at it—he was terrified of what he might see if he did. "You're going to get that fucking bullet out of my leg, and then I'll get you more water than you can drink."

"No," she said. "I'll do it, but I need some water first. My hands will shake too much if I don't have any, and you'll just get mad at me."

Hooper looked into her eyes. Not steely, that had been taken from her, but she was telling the truth. "Fine," he said, moving the plate and bottle farther from her just to be safe. "But when I get back, no more fucking around." He looked at the clock over the washing machine. It was almost 6:00 a.m.

38

Despite having snuck out the night before, Tim was the first one up in the house. He dressed quickly, walked to the kitchen, filled a water bottle from the faucet, and went outside. The sun was up, but barely, and Tim opened the garage so he could get to the equipment. He dragged the wheelbarrow and transfer shovel out of their places at the rear of the garage, then filled the wheelbarrow with pea gravel from the slowly diminishing pile and began to push the thing around the house.

Between his and his dad's trips around the garage to the site of the patio, they had managed to wear a groove from the heavy wheelbarrow into the lawn. Tim had no idea how many trips around the house they'd made, nor did he really want to. He was still shocked that he had been dragged into the whole thing. His dad had been almost impossibly cool about not treating him like a slave just because he'd been unlucky enough to happen to be born a boy and heavy lifting needed to happen. *Of course this happened. It was going to be the perfect summer; something was bound to ruin it.*

How could he bitch about having a bad summer? The thought burned a pit into Tim's stomach as he dumped the wheelbarrow's contents into the hole in the yard. Luke was living in a tree fort, some other kid had gotten killed and left at the drive-in, and Molly was still missing. His face went hot. He felt like a total jerk.

He set the much lighter wheelbarrow down, grabbed a rake that been left leaning against the house overnight, and began spreading the dumped rocks around the hole. When he was done he dropped the rake, grabbed the wheelbarrow, and walked back around to the front of the house.

This is never going to be finished.

Tim was on his tenth trip back to the pile when he rounded the house and saw his dad. "Early start?" Stan asked. "Looks like you made another dent—not bad."

Tim began filling the wheelbarrow with the shovel. "Yeah, I figured if I wasn't sleeping I may as well get to it. No time like the present, right?"

"No, I suppose you're right," said Stan. "Is the rake out back?"

"Yep, I must have missed it last night when I did cleanup. Sorry about that."

Tim didn't see it, but his dad got an odd look on his face when Tim said that, as though an idea popped into his head for the very first time. It was the sort of look that Tim would have described as weird and his mom would have said "uh-oh" about. Stan walked around the house, the look still on his face, and Tim continued filling the wheelbarrow.

When Tim had bullied the wheelbarrow back to the hole for the fifth time, he saw that his dad had strategically moved the pea gravel he'd been dumping to the corners farthest from the front of the hole. That way they wouldn't have to make the edge of the hole uneven by running the wheelbarrow in and out of it over and over again.

"I think we're almost there," said Stan, who was using the side of a level to measure the distance between the top of the gravel and the edge of the hole. "We want to leave about an inch gap, then we compress that down to two and a quarter inches and start putting in pavers. When you come back around, grab the tamper, would you?"

"What's a tamper?"

"It's the metal square with a handle sticking up from it. You'll know it when you see it. Bring it on back so we can start packing this gravel. At this rate I'll be calling to get some pavers delivered this afternoon."

Tim grabbed the now-empty wheelbarrow and brought it back around to the front of the house. He hadn't really noticed before, but he'd made a massive dent in the gravel this morning. The pile had at most three or four more loads to go. He set the wheelbarrow down, went into the garage, then walked around to the backyard with what he thought was the tamper.

"Is this it?" he asked, holding the tamper up. It weighed about twenty pounds or so, and Tim felt sure that some new and horrible labor was to be done with it.

"That would be the one. Go ahead and bring it on over. We can learn how not to screw this up together." Tim crossed the sea of loose gravel and handed the thing to his dad. It felt more like a crude club than something from the hardware store, like a modern-day mace or war hammer.

"Now, I think the basic gist of it," Stan said, "is that we use the flat end to compress the gravel."

Tim rolled his eyes. "I kind of figured that much, Dad."

Stan walked to the southernmost corner of the hole, close to the hose, and drove the tamper into the gravel five or six times, all in the same general area. "Grab that level, Tim," he said as he pushed his glasses up on his nose. Tim did, then handed it to his dad, who stuck it in the gravel and against the edge of the hole. "That just dropped it three-quarters of an inch. That's pretty crazy."

"We have to do that to all of it?" Tim asked, incredulous. Every step of building a patio seemed to be worse than the one before. As angry as he was with his dad, he couldn't help but feel bad for the guy, as well as for himself.

"Yep, that's what we have to do. Even worse, it all has to be level when we're done. You want to give it a try?"

Tim took the tamper from his dad, gave himself some space, and started pounding the pea gravel into submission.

Stan measured when Tim was done. "Not bad, another quarter inch and we're there."

"Yeah, for this spot," said Tim. "There's going to be a whole lot of 'we're theres' before we're finished."

Stan's grin at this rolled into a frown. "Tim, I was thinking about something you said in front of the house earlier. I'm not sure it's going to make a bit of difference, but I was curious. You said you were sorry for leaving the rake out back. It's a good thing about you. You always say sorry about stuff like that. In fact, I can't remember you ever not saying sorry after doing something wrong, or forgetting something, ever since you first learned your manners. You want to know what's weird about that?"

"Sure, what?" Tim said, before pounding the tamper into the gravel, imagining he had a jackhammer or some other piece of heavy machinery, instead of some modern version of what was almost undoubtedly a centuries-old tool.

"You never said sorry for lying at the police station. It never occurred to me until right now."

"I know I didn't," said Tim, speaking in between blasts of tamping the gravel down. "And I'm not going to. You and Mom can punish me as much as you want, but I'm not going to apologize for trying to help a kidnapped girl." Tim kept working, letting his anger power him and turn his upper body into a piston.

Tim didn't know it, but his dad was staring at him, looking as though he had just realized he might have made a horrible mistake.

39

Hooper lay on his stomach. Sweat was pouring off of his face and pooling on the cold concrete, and the revolver was in his hand. She had the forceps in his leg again, and in a reversal of how things had been, the ball gag was in his mouth now, though it remained unfastened. He grunted against the ball, the sounds coming from him foreign-sounding even to Hooper's own ears.

He checked the clock. They'd been at it for only five minutes.

After Hooper had brought her the water, Amy had sipped it slowly. At first he'd been frustrated—he really wanted to get this over with—but then he understood. She'd been dehydrated, perhaps even dangerously so, and she was likely scared of getting sick by drinking it too fast.

She set the glass down before it was empty and said, "So how do I do this?"

"Well, first off, I'm going to have a couple swallows from that bottle of high-test that I brought down," said Hooper. "Then you're going to pour some of it on my leg, and after the pain fades, you're going to use the knife and those fly-tying forceps to try and get that bullet out of my leg." He watched her stare at the tools on the plate for a minute and then continued. "I know what you're thinking, and don't for a minute believe I haven't considered you might try something. That's why I brought this heater down with me. You start fucking around or thinking this is a chance to escape, I will not hesitate to put a hundred-fifty-grain hollow point into your skull. Get it?"

She nodded, and he took some clean towels from atop the dryer. He set the towels on the floor next to her and then sat heavily. "Look, I know you're mad as hell and you don't want to help me. But as much as I don't want you to be the one to pull that bullet out of me, you're the only person who can. Hell, it'd be one thing if I could reach it properly, but there's no way I can do some garage surgery on myself when I can't even see what I need to be digging around in. So you got to be the one to do it, and I got to let you.

"I figure if you do a good enough job we'll both be fine, and if not, you get one in your dome and I wind up figuring out some story to tell while I'm waiting on an ambulance. I don't know if I'm a good enough liar to pull that off, but I sure as shit know you're not good enough with that little blade to stop me from shooting you if I get to thinking I need to."

Amy nodded at him. She looked onboard, as though she respected the situation and knew that doing a good job would benefit her just as much as it would him. It was sort of like dangling a carrot in front of a mule, Hooper thought. It was a good trick, but not a fair one. The only thing that was going to be happening for little old Amy once he got put back together was a whole lot of fucking. Maybe she'd come to see that was what would keep her alive, and maybe she wouldn't, but just like with extracting the bullet, it was going to happen.

He drank two quick swallows of the grain alcohol, shivering both times as the shitty-tasting liquid scorched his palate. Hooper didn't care for strong drink. Life could be difficult enough without going around cutting your wits in half with booze, and it had been years since he'd had so much as a beer. Still, it seemed to be a necessary evil to dull if not completely shut off his senses.

He handed Amy the bottle and said, "Pour some on the wound, then dry it with one of those towels." She took the bottle, Hooper took a deep breath, and then fire was racing up his leg all over again.

"It's really swollen," said Amy. "Are you sure you want to do this? I don't want you to shoot me just because it hurts."

She was gingerly wiping off his leg while she spoke, and when she was done, Hooper emptied his lungs and said, "You'll be fine, girl. Just don't go getting cute. I figure what you ought to do is open that hole back up with the knife and then go digging for the bullet with those forceps. If you stick to that plan, we'll be doing just fine."

"When do you want me to start?"

"There's no time like the present," said Hooper, and she began to cut. He added the ball gag to his mouth just a few seconds later. The feeling of her cutting into his wounded skin was just about the worst thing he'd ever experienced.

"There's like, black blood coming out," said Amy. "It's thicker than blood, and it's really gross. There's some yellow stuff leaking out too. Are you sure we need to do this?"

"That just means we should have done it yesterday," said Hooper, after spitting the gag into his hand. He sure didn't envy Amy's having to wear it all the time. "Have you cut it enough yet?"

She hesitated, then said, "No, at least I don't think so. This knife isn't very sharp—"

Hooper cut her off. "It's going to have to work. Just put your back into it and get it over with. I can't do this all day."

She started cutting in earnest then, and Hooper slid the saliva-slick ball back into his mouth and chomped down on it. And again the pain was somehow worse still than anything he'd ever felt. Worse than getting shot, worse than shrapnel had been, worse than falling off his bike when he was nine and breaking his arm.

"Done," said Amy, after what felt like an eternity. "At least I think we are. The hole is big enough now that I think the forceps will fit. How will I know when I get to the bullet?"

Hooper had to pant for a while before he could talk. "You'll feel it," he said at last. "It'll be like tapping metal on metal."

"All right," said Amy, sounding utterly unconvinced. "Here goes, OK?" When she was done speaking Hooper felt the forceps enter him, and he nearly swooned from the pain. Somehow, it was worse than even the cutting had been. The ball gag fell from his mouth to the cement floor, forgotten, at least for the moment. Looking over his shoulder, Hooper could see her working. The forceps were in his leg, several inches deep at least. The yellow pus, or whatever it was, made it look like a longtime smoker had blown a loogie full of snot and throat stones all over the back of his leg. He was surprised to see that aside from the pus and black coagulate, there was little fluid coming from the wound, and what was coming out was thin and looked diluted to his untrained eyes.

"Do you feel anything yet?" Hooper asked, his voice a wreck.

"No," said Amy. "But there's a lot more of that yellow stuff coming out. It's really gross and it stinks super bad." Hooper had smelled something foul through the pain but had been trying to ignore it. Now that he was fully aware of that awful odor, he rec-ognized the smell. It was the stench of death. *Thank God we're get-ting it out now and didn't wait any longer.* The sensation of being stabbed made his eyes water and shocked his vision into black spots. Hooper took a deep breath, then opened his eyes and raised the gun. He was looking down the sights at the top of Amy's head, expecting to find her jabbing away with the knife, intent on killing him, but she wasn't. She was crouched in her filthy bra and under-wear—something else that would need attention—with blood covering her hands, and she was digging away with the forceps.

Hooper felt his mind starting to clear, and thank goodness—he'd almost just shot her, and all she was doing was what he'd told her to do. He lowered the gun. She hadn't even noticed how close he'd just come to killing her.

Hooper laid his head back down on the cement floor, trying to establish a rhythm of breathing, hoping that it would help keep him from further swooning or delirium. Suddenly there was a pain worse than anything, worse than being shot or cut. Hooper was scared he was going to break a tooth, when Amy exclaimed, "I got it!"

Hooper felt a warmth rush over his leg, and he began to crawl away from her. He was dizzier than before, but he had the sense to grab a pair of the towels as he crawled, as well as to hang on to the gun. He wrapped the towels around his leg—it hurt to even know that it was attached to him, much worse to touch it. He had moved as far from her as he could when he heard chopper blades in the night, as well as a young girl screaming for help. Hooper fell into the black.

40

"I'm going to lose my shield over this," said Van Endel. "I know it."

It was late afternoon, and he was sitting in Dr. Martinez's office, blowing off steam. The trail following Molly Peterson was only a few days old, but it didn't matter. Between the body still in the morgue with its lack of clues, and the lack of a dental report, the case was dead in the water. There was no evidence, no witnesses forthcoming. Van Endel had been over the notes so many times that he'd all but memorized exactly what all of the teenagers, boys, and movie theater employees had told him. They'd had the local news affiliates run pieces saying that they were looking for information from anyone who'd been to the drive-in the night Molly disappeared, and it had proven to be a colossal waste of time. There had been plenty of people there, all had seen teens, and none could confirm whether or not Molly and her friends had been there.

"You're not going to lose your badge over this," said Dr. Martinez. "And the GRPD is going to keep working with me. This isn't our fault, not any more than the Riverside murders are. Whoever left that body there meant for the trail to die, and they achieved that goal. The fact of the matter is, that probably was Molly, and we aren't going to catch the guy who left her there unless he does something very stupid, like trying to grab another victim from the drive-in anytime soon."

It was true. From talking to the owner of the outdoor movie theater, they'd learned that a dead teenager found just off the premises had not been good for business, nor had the general assumption that she had been taken from the place. A large memorial had bloomed up at the entrance to the drive-in: flowers, crosses, teddy bears, pictures of Molly. The owner had complained about that too. It was an eyesore, but if he took it down he'd be a pariah. Van Endel had told him he was right, he couldn't take it down, but had to fight back peals of laughter as he'd done it. It wasn't funny, but had he felt like something in his head was starting to split, and the laughter was a symptom of it.

"OK, the drive-in is over," said Van Endel. "What do you propose I do next? I've already considered reinterviewing the teenagers who were with her, but I don't see it going anywhere. They had nothing for me the morning after she was taken, they're not going to do any better now. If they were over eighteen I could try and break one of them, but none of them have committed a crime, not a severe one anyways. If I get tough—"

"Then the parents just lawyer up," said Dr. Martinez. "I get it. Still, there has to be something out there. Someone has to have seen something."

"That's what I would have thought, but think about what we know about Riverside. Drives a green car—maybe. Is a white male who favors a ball cap and glasses. Of course, we were also told by pretty much every hooker on Division Avenue that they've been picked up by a guy with that exact description and came back A-OK to get back to business."

"And because most of them return just fine, they'll still get in green cars with white males," said Dr. Martinez wearily. "And the ones who don't aren't noticed until we come around asking questions and showing off pictures."

"Exactly," said Van Endel. "There's not much left on this one for either of us to do." Van Endel chuckled to himself, and Dr. Martinez gave him a quizzical look. "It's funny. If those kids—the three boys, not the teens—really had been telling the truth, we'd have tons of people to talk to."

Dr. Martinez shrugged. "You have to follow the evidence, right? And the available evidence says you need to assume the teens are telling the truth and the boys are lying. That said, you know my feelings on the matter. Body or not, not one of those boys came off to me as a liar."

"At least you like it as much as I do," said Van Endel. "This is just infuriating. There's a young girl missing, dead most likely, and there's not a damn thing we can do about it."

"Well," said Martinez, "there is the hope that Tracy finally gets a negative on those teeth. If that's not Molly, those boys might really have seen her."

"Yeah, I know," said Van Endel. "I've had that thought at least a million times. Not ideal conditions for grabbing a decent night's sleep. Hey, that reminds me. I didn't tell you what Tracy found on the body. I don't think much of it, but he thought it was interesting." Dr. Martinez tilted her head, as if to say, "Go on." "She had condoms on her. More than just one too, though Tracy couldn't tell me exactly how many. Think it means anything other than that she wanted to party?"

"That's interesting," said Dr. Martinez. "Did the mother give any indication that Molly was sexually active?"

Van Endel shrugged. "Mothers aren't necessarily the best source for that info, as you know. But as it happens, this one made it a point to tell me that her daughter was not sexually active. I can't remember the exact quote, but it was something like, 'She does stuff with boys, but not *that*.' She was almost smug about it.

Molly was either telling the truth or lying well enough that her mom believed her."

"You know," said Dr. Martinez. "Molly has something in common with those girls who keep showing up at Riverside, other than being missing, of course." Van Endel raised his eyebrows. "Rubbers, Dick. Every single working girl on Division Avenue has them on her."

"I have a picture of Molly in my car," said Van Endel. "Let's go for a ride." He looked at his watch. "It's a little early, but we should be able to catch some day shifters."

41

Luke was walking through the neighborhood doing something he never had before: actually analyzing what was around him. It had never occurred to him before that he spent so much time whizzing around on a bicycle or fighting imaginary battles that he had never really focused on the people around him, and the myriad differences in the ways they lived. Tim had told them that Becca had said to look for things like an unmowed lawn, and Luke was trying to take that a step further, looking for windowless vans, poorly maintained landscaping, and signs that said KIDNAPPER posted in someone's front yard. He'd seen lots of yards that needed mowing, several windowless vans, and a great number of homes with poorly kept landscaping, but he was batting zero on KIDNAPPER signs.

This is a total waste of time, thought Luke as he walked on a street perpendicular to the one that Scott lived on, and actually bordered the woods where the fort was. So far he had seen two houses that stuck out: one a couple of blocks from here, also along the forest's edge, and one that was gray and needed paint. Beside the latter, Luke had seen a man in an unbuttoned Hawaiian shirt watering a dying bush with a hose. The man had been on crutches and looked to be of a similar build as the one they'd seen in the woods, though he had a gut Luke didn't remember seeing.

He wished Scott and Tim were with him, and not for the first time. It would be nice to have someone to talk to, and to ask questions about how they remembered the man looking.

The other house that had stuck out as being a little off had many of the same characteristics as the first one, though there was no injured owner visible to add more weight to the picture it painted. The house was made of red bricks and was small enough that Luke couldn't imagine anyone other than a single man or woman living in it. The yard was unmowed, and the grass had yellow and dead patches, even with the rainy spring and June that they'd had that year. In addition to the ratty yard, the car in the driveway was an ancient El Camino. It was black but looked like it had been painted with a roller or something, and there were several dried spots of black, too dark to be oil, in the driveway around the car.

What made the house stick out most of all, though, was the impression it gave of having somehow been taken from another neighborhood and just transplanted there. There were no other brick houses on that stretch, and it didn't fit the mold that all of the houses on the same strip seemed to come from. The rest of the houses were ranch-style, with attached garages and aluminum siding. Families were outside most of the other houses, messing around and lighting off small fireworks, but the little brick house had no one outside.

Luke had forgotten all about the Fourth until he'd been out on his little recon mission, but the signs of it were everywhere: blackened fountains and cakes lined the bases of driveways, sticks from bottle rockets littered the road and yards, little kids ran around with sparklers and snap-pops. It made Luke homesick in a way that he hadn't been since this had all happened. He wasn't telling his friends about his trips to the gas station to buy food during the day, or about what it was like not having his crazy mother and sisters around. Frankly, it was sweet as hell, but there was also a sadness lingering over him that he knew wasn't going away.

He felt like a traitor for thinking it, but Luke had a feeling that this was all going to blow over, and without anything happening. Molly was going to be found dead, or maybe one of his friends would get caught sneaking out, and then that would be it. There would be no clearing their names, just a stigma that was going to follow him through the rest of middle school, and maybe on into high school. It would follow his friends too, but it would be different for them. After all, everything else outside of school was different for them; it was only a matter of time until his school world caught up. He would no longer be just another student. He'd be that trailer-park liar, or some other, equally awful version of that, in the eyes of his fellow students and his teachers. That part almost stung the most: knowing that for the foreseeable future, adults were always going to assume that he could be lying to them. The thought fueled Luke as he pushed on through the suburb, finding clues that didn't matter and looking for answers that weren't going to reveal themselves.

The house appeared before him only moments after his self-defeating train of thought had eked away the last of his interest in searching for it. He almost didn't notice it. It had its back to the forest, and the backyard was fully encompassed by a tall wooden fence. Neither of the houses on either side of it was two stories, so the backyard would be basically impossible to see into. Luke could see that the fence went almost all the way to the trees.

Cutting through the yard of a neighbor a couple of doors down, he looped around into the forest and quickly came upon a cluster of popples that looked quite similar to the one the man and Molly had disappeared into. He spent some time trying to orient himself to where the fort would be in relation to where he was standing. Unless he was mistaken, Luke was pretty sure this house was in exactly the direction they'd seen the man and Molly walking.

He cut back to the street and gave one last look to the mailbox. The address was stenciled on it, and above it the word HOOPER.

Luke headed back to the fort at a dead run.

42

Tim and his dad had finished tamping down about ten square feet of gravel when Stan sat down on the edge of the patio. "Go get Mom," he said. "I want to see if she'll be impressed with our progress yet. We're finally getting places, thanks to your early start."

Tim left his dad and the tamper behind him but brought the water bottle along for the trip. The ache in his arms stayed with him, though, as he slowly walked around and then into the house through the open garage door. "Mom," he called as he walked inside and kicked off his shoes. "Dad wants you to go outside and look at the ground."

"Did he finish it?" his mom asked from the kitchen. "It'd be amazing if he did—we haven't even had the pavers delivered yet!"

"Not yet," Tim said, walking to the sink and dumping out what was left of the water in his bottle, "but we're making progress." He turned the sink to cold and let it run for a minute before refilling the bottle.

His mom was doing some prep work on dinner, or at least that's how it looked to Tim as he sat at the table. He considered getting himself a snack but decided that a moment to sit trumped the growing hunger pangs in his belly.

Tammy washed her hands, then dried them on a towel before walking out through the garage. She had to go the long way around too, since the slider and the patio were out of service.

Alone in the house, Tim remembered Becca. He stood, then crept to her room, as though on some sort of clandestine mission. When he knocked on her door, Becca made some neutral sound that wasn't a no, and he walked inside.

Becca was reading again, the same book as before, but when she saw it was him she dropped it in her lap and stared at him. "What do you want?"

"Mom and Dad are both outside. Can you call whoever was with Molly when she was taken?"

Becca narrowed her eyes. "Are you sure I'll have time? I really don't need Mom any further up my ass."

"Yes, I'm positive. Just hurry! I'll go stand by the door as a lookout."

"Fair enough," she sighed. "But you better let me know if they're coming, because I'm going to be on the phone in their room. That's like double trouble if I get busted." Tim looked at her quizzically, and she rolled her eyes. "Jesus, sometimes I wonder if we're really related. I can't use the kitchen phone. Mom would be able to see me from outside. Now get out of my room and go watch the door."

Tim ran toward the door to the garage. *We're just lucky Mom can't use the slider like normal, because of the patio.* He smiled, the first time he'd done that since his work on the never-ending project had started. It was finally good for something.

Tim stood waiting by the back of the family room, where he had a good view of the door from the garage. For what felt like an eternity he waited for the sound of the knob turning, or for Becca to appear and tell him that it was done. He felt weird, some-how both tense and sleepy. He was wondering if maybe this was how high schoolers felt during exams, or how his dad felt grading exams, when he heard Becca walking from their parents' bedroom to her own at almost the exact same moment the knob to the garage door started to turn. He slipped down the hall into the bathroom, in case his mom checked for him, and when he heard her in the kitchen again he darted off to Becca's room.

He opened the door without knocking, slid inside, and closed it after him. "Well?"

"It was a dark green Dodge Dart, the Colombia model. Jeff, one of the guys who saw her get in, remembered." While Tim was repeating that to himself—*dark green Dodge Dart, Colombia model*—Becca went on talking, probably stir-crazy from being grounded. "Jeff's a pretty good guy, but…Did I tell you I'm kind of scared to hang out with anybody from that crowd again? It's a total bummer, like, I busted ass to get in with the cool kids, and they seem pretty stupid in retrospect."

"I'm glad you could help. Same for your friend," said Tim, once he was sure he had the car's make and model down. "But what you guys did, and then didn't do, was pretty awful. Ripping off a bunch of jerks is one thing, but then you lied to the cops, even when one of your friends was in trouble." He stood.

"So what now?" Becca asked, but like she was only mildly interested. Tim wondered if she'd heard anything he'd said.

"Now I think we have to find that car, and then…Well, after that, I don't know."

"Just don't do anything stupid, OK? And keep us out of it. How about just an anonymous phone call telling them about the car?"

Tim scoffed at that. "There's no way they'd believe it. That Van Endel guy is so used to getting lied to, or at least thinking he's getting lied to, that I doubt he'd even follow up. And if he did, whoever has her would just lie his way out of it if the cops did stop by. Not that they would. They probably made like a million of that car."

Becca frowned. "I can't recall seeing many of them, not around here, anyway." She paused, then cocked her head as if realizing something. "Do you think Mom and Dad will let us go see the fireworks?"

"I don't know," said Tim. "But it won't matter too much. Everybody lights them off all over the place anyways. Either way, we'll get a show."

43

Hooper woke up stuck to the floor. His leg had soaked through the towels, and it now felt as though an industrial-strength adhesive had been used to bind him to the cement. Amy was either asleep on her side or pretending to be asleep. Not that it mattered now—Hooper had no use for her at the moment. As bad as he felt, she couldn't have been more useless. He grabbed the gun, ignoring the plate and the bottle of Everclear for now, and then tried to stand.

His leg came free of the floor slowly, making a sound like a giant zipper as it parted ways with the cement. A hot, fresh wave of pain blasted off the wound. Without touching it, Hooper waved a hand near it and felt a palpable heat rising from it. Holding on to the wall near the stairs, he tested his weight on the leg. It would work, barely. He knelt, then slowly extended his arm so he wouldn't fall, and grabbed the ball gag. He stood again, then hopped on his good leg over to the pole that Amy was tied to. Once there, he slid down and then slipped the gag into her mouth. She stirred but did not wake as he attached the harness and then tightened. He seemed to recall her yelling out for help, but he could have been wrong. The memory of the basement surgery flashed back at him, and then a darker cloud ran through his mind. That kid or possibly even kids in the woods.

Hooper might not have been well enough at the moment to go after them, but he smiled, imagining himself with two healthy legs. The smile didn't last long, though, as there came a thunderous explosion from outside. Hooper scrambled, pain be damned, to the window. What he saw took his breath away. *Fuckin' Charlie is fuckin' bombing the goddamn town!* There could be no other explanation; mortar bursts were erupting throughout the night sky, exploding shrapnel in deadly glory, exactly like the shrapnel that had nearly killed him back in the shit, back in the jungle.

Hooper ducked as a shot roared up from somewhere impossibly close to the house and exploded with precision next to it. Something in his mind popped, and he fell to the ground, shaking in a violent dance on the floor.

Some minutes later, he forced himself to sit up, cringing at the sound of the bombs bursting in the air. His injured leg was literally trembling, pulsing with his beating heart. Scared to look at it, but knowing he had to, Hooper began to turn his head, then stopped when he saw the stretch marks mottling the swollen skin. Scrabbling like a drunken crab, he began spinning on the floor, taken by madness and pain and screaming inaudibly at the same moment a mortar exploded and the back of his leg rubbed on the floor. The shock was too great. He expelled urine and shit from his body in a great flood and then lay in it, morbidly cooling off as the mess of fluids gave away the heat it had gained in his body.

Hooper lay there for a long time. As terrible as the endless barrage was, he seemed to be safe. The ground wasn't rumbling like it had back in the shit, and no one was screaming in pain from shrapnel, like he had been on that awful night of fire and lead. *No one came for me then, and they won't now, either.* Help hadn't come until the next morning; those pussy medics had had to wait until the area was clear to come get him. The men around Hooper had died slowly, their screams sputtering out like motors running out of fuel. *Not again, not again*, thought Hooper, a moment of clarity allowing him to see the filth he was lying in. The moment begged for another, and Hooper all but dragged himself to his feet, his injured leg leaking blood and pus as he dragged it behind him to the bathroom, his foot turned sideways and the leg dying the slow death of rot.

Hooper turned on the shower, then all but fell in. He was in a boat racing up a Vietnamese river, but he shook the false thought away. Hooper had never been upriver, downriver, or on any river that wasn't in Michigan. Still, the memory had come from somewhere, and it felt real enough. He slowly lowered himself to a sitting position in the shower, tearing off the curtain and landing on his ass with just a few inches to go. He threw the curtain aside and let the shower work its magic of cleaning his mind and body. Slowly the shit, piss, blood, and pus were scraped off of him by the slowly warming stream, and it felt wonderful, the best feeling in the world.

Clarity came to Hooper in violent waves, memories from the shit interspersed with movie memories that seemed more and less real at the same time. Also in there were thick blasts of Amy, both the new and the old one. Amy before Vietnam, wearing high-cut denim shorts and laughing with her friends outside in the driveway. Hooper brooding in the house as his mom wheezed and fucking groaned on her respirator. That same Amy moaning beneath him, or was it crying? It hadn't mattered then, but it seemed to now, for some reason. The new Amy came to him then, Amy strapped to the pole, begging for water. What had he fed her in the last few days? Three or four pieces of dried toast, a few glasses of water? *The bitch deserves it*, another voice said plainly. *She ran, she let that VC motherfucker shoot you.* Another seizure wracked Hooper, and he danced the sleep of the dying in the bathtub, every noise but a death rattle escaping his body.

The cold woke him up violently, helped along with the pain from his leg. He was no longer being blasted by the shock of the pain. It came in waves now, attacking his nervous system like the barrages the VC kept throwing at his long-ago-destroyed emplacement. He knew that risk was past, that he'd been home for years, but every single Fourth of July explosion told him otherwise, each blast a death knell for the men around him, who were a mix of shadows, screams, and spilled blood. Hooper shouted with them, adding his own voice to the raucous sounds of a world gone mad. History and the present were flashing back and forth in ugly intervals, wounds suffered long ago finding a place alongside those of the present. Hooper lay in the shower, letting the water run over him as though it could make him pure.

44

The afternoon had yielded no hits, and Van Endel was starting to think the holiday might have cut down on the night trade. He was wrong, though, and was almost depressed over it. Even hookers deserved a day off, but from the look of things, most of them had decided that dusk on the Fourth of July was still a perfectly fine time to offer their wares.

Van Endel and Martinez had circled the blocks where the women were most apt to be walking. The men's district was a little farther north, though the job opportunities were basically the same. Finally, Martinez spotted a woman they'd talked to before, a rough-looking black hooker who said her name was Candy. "Hard Candy," she'd told them—if a john got too pushy or tried not to pay, that is. Van Endel pulled the car to the curb and let Martinez get out first, then followed her. Women tended to make them less jumpy, doubly so after the last eighteen months of steady disappearances.

"Is that Candy?" Dr. Martinez called out, in a voice that was almost as much a lie as the girl's name. "I know that's my girl Candy. You remember me?"

"I don't know you, White Bread," said Candy. "Now get the fuck out of here."

Van Endel was between the two women almost immediately, holding his badge in one hand and the picture of Molly in the other.

"Candy, I know you recognize us," said Van Endel. "I'm the detective that you hate talking to. *I'm* white bread. Dr. Martinez here is more of a tortilla in ethnicity, and her you like, if you recall correctly."

"Oh shit, Doc," said Candy. "I'm sorry, I didn't mean no harm, but you looked like this white bitch from some church that's been buggin' the shit out of us lately, and chasing away the money and the men too. She could keep the men, but the money, that's a problem," said Candy with a smile so vivid and full of life that it was almost heartbreaking. Van Endel didn't figure she gave that look to too many people, and it was sweet enough to take some of the hard living off of her face.

"I need to ask you some questions, Candy," said Dr. Martinez, taking the picture of Molly from Van Endel and slipping back in front of him. She handed the photo to the working girl. "This girl's named Molly Peterson, and she's been missing for almost five days. The detective and I are trying to find her. Can you help us?"

"Probably not," said Candy. "She don't look like no girl that would be down here. She look like she still in school. She could make some money, though. She's pretty enough."

"All right," said Dr. Martinez. "We felt like this was kind of a long shot to come down here, but it was nice to see—"

"Hold on," said Van Endel. A thought had struck deep as an ice pick into his brain. "Have you heard of anything weird happening down here with any high school kids? Not the usual things, like being assholes and throwing garbage around, but just sort of being around?"

"Actually, yeah," said Candy. She paused, and Dr. Martinez made a ten-dollar bill disappear in Candy's hand. "Yeah, now that

I remember it, another girl workin' these streets, Bambi, told me she saw a shitload of teenagers out here fuckin' around a few days ago. Not like fuckin' with the girls or johns or nothin', just fuckin' around and shit. You know, like kids."

"Where does Bambi work usually?" Van Endel asked, trying to mask the elation in his voice. *We might actually be getting somewhere, so relax, don't blow it.*

"She usually over by Cherry, like a block back that way," said Candy, then held her hands up. "But I ain't helping you find her. I gots to make money, and I don't need to be seen with no police. No offense, Dr. Martinez."

"None taken, Candy," said Dr. Martinez with a smile. "Before we let you get back to work, can you tell us what Bambi looks like, how she usually dresses?"

"I'll tell you how she look, but you don't need to worry about how she dress. You'll know her as soon as you see her. She pretty as hell, even for a pale-ass white girl. She tall, almost six foot, and she wears them heels that'll break your leg if you ain't careful. She got long, almost white hair, and she keeps it in braids."

"All right," said Dr. Martinez, slipping Candy another ten-dollar bill. "Thank you for your help."

"Shit, Doc, thanks. You know, since you being so cool and all, even if you travel with bad company, watch out for Bambi's man. I don't know if he's all pimp or just a guy who rents his lady, but he's a mean son of a bitch. Shit, if he didn't mark her up so bad, she'd make more money."

Dr. Martinez gave Candy a wave as she got in the car, then saw a frowning Van Endel as she sat. "Is there a problem?"

"Not yet there isn't," said Van Endel. "I just want you to make sure that you follow my lead if we find this girl. If I tell you to get back in the car, or to get down, I'm not doing it to show off. If this boyfriend is even half the asshole Candy says he is, I want to make sure we're both ready to deal with him."

"All right. I can do that."

They saw what had to be Bambi less than fifteen minutes later, and did the same thing as before. Dr. Martinez came first, followed by Van Endel, who had already unsnapped his holster. Bambi looked exactly as Candy had described her. She was wearing impossibly tall stiletto heels, had nearly white braids down to her backside, and was very clearly strung out on something. Had Van Endel been forced to guess, based on the lack of visible sores on her arms and legs, he would have guessed cocaine.

"Can I have a word, Bambi?" Dr. Martinez asked. "I need to know if you've seen a friend of mine."

"Get the fuck away from me," said Bambi. "I'm trying to work, bitch. Go talk about Jesus to somebody who gives a shit." She turned quickly, and impressively, considering the footwear, but Dr. Martinez circled ahead of her. Van Endel kept pace, his hand in his jacket, his fingers on the butt of the Glock 17 he carried. Van Endel had taken shit for his dismissal of the typical wheel gun most cops carried, at least at first. Once the other officers had seen what he could do with it on the range, though, a number of them had switched to the Austrian semiauto.

"I just need a second," Dr. Martinez assured Bambi. "I have money. All you need to do is answer a couple of questions for me. Five minutes, tops, OK?"

"Or I could run you in for solicitation," said Van Endel, appearing behind Dr. Martinez with his badge out. "I'd rather just have you answer a couple of questions, though, OK? Nobody has to go to jail. We talk, and then we leave and you go back to what you do." The girl's eyes twitched to the left, where Van Endel had noticed an alley when he parked. He spun, getting his body between whatever was coming and Martinez, and his pistol free of the holster.

Van Endel ducked under the blow from the baseball bat and shoved Dr. Martinez aside, nearly toppling her. The man swinging it was obviously doped out of his mind. His eyes were dull and sunken, and he bore the ghastly pallor and racist tattoos of a neo-Nazi junkie who didn't like the outdoors too much. Van Endel punched him in the stomach with a left, doubling the skinhead up, and then brought the Glock down on his head, easing up a bit at the last second. Nonetheless, Van Endel pushed the barrel into the idiot's head plenty hard, dropping him to his knees. "Stay down on the ground," he barked, and the man did. Van Endel knelt on him, pushing his knee hard into the junkie's back, then cuffed him. "You stay there, got it, asshole?" The man grunted, and Van Endel stood before reholstering the pistol. It had taken only a few seconds.

"Make her talk," Van Endel said to Dr. Martinez. "Ask nicely if you have to, but make clear that if she doesn't soon, I'm making a call."

"You heard him, honey," said Dr. Martinez to Bambi. "Can we have a conversation?"

The girl gave a look to the now-docile man on the ground, the one who probably forced her out here, kept her on drugs, and told her he loved her after the occasional beating. "I can try," said Bambi. "Not like I have a choice."

"You're right," said Dr. Martinez. "You don't, so we may as well get started. Word is you might have seen some folks who didn't fit the neighborhood all that well a couple days ago." She held up the picture of Molly. "Is this one of them?"

"I saw some kids, sure," said Bambi. "But I never got much of a look at them, and I don't really know what they were up to. Not for sure, anyways. I mean, you hear things, but—"

"Let's see what you got on your person, playboy," Van Endel said, kneeling next to the boyfriend/pimp. He rifled through one front pocket and then the other, careful to avoid the old junkie trick of a vertical needle above the stash, point up. The second pocket revealed a couple of small and mostly empty baggies, with traces of a white dust, Van Endel figured either cocaine or speed. "Now we've got a problem. Either you tell your girlfriend to start spitting out the truth, or we're going downtown. Don't let the suit fool you—I've walked a beat, and I know the look a junkie gets when he thinks he might get a spot in a cage."

"Just fucking tell him!" screamed the idiot on the ground, and had he not been yelling exactly what Van Endel wanted to hear, he might've received a kick to the ribs.

"Your call," said Dr. Martinez to Bambi.

"All right, fine," she said. "But I already pretty much told you everything. Some suburb kids were out fucking around. I don't know for sure what they were doing—"

"I love a good rumor," said Dr. Martinez. "Spill it, Bambi. Everything you heard. My friend and I are very good bullshit detectors."

"OK," said Bambi. "I heard there were some kids going around scamming johns. I couldn't tell you for sure what they were doing, but what I heard was that there were some chicks that might have been working, but might not have been, really. Like, they were acting like hookers but were setting up guys to get robbed. I can't prove any of it, and I won't testify or anything. This is just all stuff I heard. Can't believe half what you hear. Everybody's been talking and talking, with all these girls turning up killed. And then this other girl goes missing."

Van Endel was a little surprised. "You heard about our high school girl? Our missing Molly?" He held up Molly's picture again.

Bambi gave him a look. "Molly who? I don't know any Molly high school girl. I'm talking about Shelly. She's a friend of mine."

"Shelly who?"

"I don't know Shelly who, I just know she's my friend and she disappeared that night. Shelly's her real name, but she goes by Angel. She went missing, but nobody knows anything but that they saw her get in a green car. You know what *that* means."

"I do," said Van Endel. "I know all about that. What did she look like?"

"A little like the girl in your picture, only not as pretty." She laughed. "The streets are rough, you know? She was short, way shorter than me—"

"About five three, dark hair, one hundred twenty pounds or so?"

Bambi shrugged. "That's Shelly, but that's a lot of girls. Why, though? You find her? Did someone hurt her? Did he hurt her?"

Van Endel shook his head. "We haven't found Shelly, no. Or at least she better hope we haven't."

"One last question," said Dr. Martinez to Bambi. "Sorry if it seems like an odd one. Do you know if Shelly keeps condoms on her, or does she go bareback?"

"No one sane goes bareback," said Bambi flatly. She spared a look to the man on the ground. It wasn't kind, but he didn't see it. "You have to be careful. It's not the 1970s, now that AIDS is around everywhere. Shelly keeps rubbers in a little black wallet in her back pocket, like, all the time. She gets the big ones, with foil. Johns like that. I've got mine right here in my purse, the same kind." She smiled sadly. "These are gold-foil wrapped, supposed to be for big dicks. Far as I can tell, they fit little dicks the same way."

45

Tim sat in the driveway, watching the fireworks with his mom, dad, and Becca. They could see the ones from the high school and the ball field well enough, and the alternating blasts of the two were a nice reminder that even with everything else going on, some things could still be normal. Despite his raging issues with them, Tim was happy to see his parents sitting together closely and with clasped hands. After all, it was far better than the alternative.

There was nothing too exciting about being outside under the stars and the explosions, but it had been such an odd week that to have something happening that felt so normal was almost a treat. He and Becca had had a brief interval of privacy when their parents were both outside looking at the hole where the patio was to be laid, but she hadn't mentioned the phone call from earlier again. In fact, she'd acted as though he wasn't in the room with her. Tim had the feeling that Becca really just wanted the whole thing to go away, that maybe for her Molly's being gone was just how things were now. He didn't like thinking that of his sister. Her coldness had always felt to him like more of a symptom of being a teenager than like an actual part of her personality, but now he wasn't so sure.

Becca should have wanted to know what else they'd discovered. She should have wondered about how he and his friends were still talking while under house arrest. She didn't appear to care, though, and Tim was pretty sure that all she really gave a crap about was her life being normal again, as if that were even possible. Everything was spiraling further and further out of control, or at least that was how it felt to Tim, and as much as he wanted to just have everything go back to normal, he knew that looking for a green Dodge Dart was far more important. He couldn't wait for the fireworks to stop so that they could all go to bed and he could see his friends again.

Finally, the explosions from the professional barrages reached a crescendo, first at the ball field, and then at the school. Smaller, private fireworks were still being launched, of course, but Tim knew what the big ones' being done really meant. Sure enough, his dad said, "All right, gang, let's head on in. Show's over." Tim hid the smile on his face. He couldn't wait to be free again, a ghost with only one purpose, loose in the night.

Tim went through the motions of brushing his teeth and washing his face, then walked to his bedroom. When he walked in, he was startled to see his dad waiting on him. "Is everything OK?" Tim asked, utterly sure that his dad had somehow discovered his nocturnal missions.

"Everything's fine," said Stan, waving a hand to Tim's bed. Tim sat where he'd been directed, and his dad did too. "I need to ask you something," said Stan. "I'd like to think I can expect you to tell me the truth, but if you don't, it's going to be on you, OK?"

"All right," said Tim. "I'm not going to lie to you."

Stan sighed and ran his fingers through his thinning hair. "Were you telling that cop the truth?"

"Yes," said Tim. "We told him the truth about everything. But we've been over this. Why are you asking me again? Am I just going to get in trouble for it all over?"

"I'm asking because I've been feeling like a real asshole. And despite how you might feel about our little situation, I don't actually enjoy coming off like that to you."

Stan took a breath, then said, "I know you never met my dad, but you didn't miss out on much. He drank too much, hit my mom, hit me, spent his whole life not trusting anyone and not liking anything. The whole reason I wanted kids in the first place was to prove to myself that I didn't need to be like him, that I could break that ugly pattern. I always felt like I was doing an OK job of that until this week. Between the crap your sister pulled and what happened with you at the police station...It's all been a little much.

"But what I keep going back to was you looking so shocked when that detective didn't believe you. The look on your face, as well as the way I reacted. At the time, I thought that you looked shocked that you got caught, but now I'm not so sure. I think maybe you were shocked that they said they'd found the body, and that you were telling the truth, or at least what you thought was the truth, the whole time. I'm going to talk to your mom about it tonight, and depending on what she says, maybe we can figure out a reduced sentence."

Tim nodded. "Dad, here's the thing. You know me. Why would I make up a lie like that? It wouldn't do me any good, and I'd get caught for sure. Plus, it would mess up the cops when they were trying to do their jobs. It's not like I have some crazy history of making up ridiculous lies."

"I've thought about all of that, Tim. Over and over again. Like I said, I'll talk to Mom, and we'll see what she has to say now that she's had the chance to cool off for a few days, all right?"

"Dad, listen. Unless you guys decide that you believe me, I don't even want to not be grounded anymore. I'd rather just do the punishment and know, for sure, that you guys don't trust me anymore."

Stan stood, shook his head like he was trying to clear water from it, and walked to the doorway. "We'll see you in the morning," he said. "Hopefully your mom will come around."

"Sure," said Tim, but all he could think was that if he got caught sneaking out, being believed wasn't going to matter one bit. Still, it could be worse. He felt sure that it was for Molly.

46

Van Endel and Dr. Martinez had talked to three more prostitutes, all with varying degrees of success. None had helped as much as Bambi, but they had helped fill in the gaps of her story. They told the same tale. Van Endel felt sick after hearing the words over and over again. *We missed it, we missed all of it.* He saved himself one indignity: he didn't puke as they left the city to head north, back to the station. Finally, Dr. Martinez broke the silence.

"You can beat yourself up all you want," she said. "But you have to wait until later. You need a plan. What are you going to tell Chief Jefferson?"

"I'm going to tell him the truth," said Van Endel. "We need to get those kids on the horn right now and see what they have to say. First the boys they saw Molly, and then later, the teenagers. The sooner it happens, the better, for everyone. Christ, even for us. I can't believe we didn't make those boys go over the story again. We should have talked to all three, tried to wring out any small details that were there to be found. If only—"

"You need to stop," said Dr. Martinez. "You've been busting your ass on this, and for that matter so have I. My practice could use a little more attention than I've been giving it, believe me, but all I've wanted to do is bang my head against this with you, and that's exactly what we've both been doing.

"And besides: even if you'd wanted to keep after those kids, there's no way Jefferson would have wanted to hear it, not after finding that body. Everything pointed to those boys' lying. There's no one who thought otherwise." She shrugged. "Now we have the chance to do something about it."

"So you think this is right?" Van Endel asked, his hands tight and sweaty on the steering wheel. "You think this is for real?"

"I do," said Dr. Martinez. "I think we have most of the puzzle put together. All that's left is to find Molly and whoever took her, and of course pray that she's still alive. Can you imagine the state she must be in if she's still alive and was taken by Riverside?"

"No," said Van Endel with a grimace. "I really can't."

Once they were back in the station, which was running on a skeleton crew, thanks to the holiday, Van Endel headed for his desk and his long-abused chair. Dr. Martinez borrowed a neighboring chair from one of the other desks and sat next to him as he dialed Jefferson's pager number. A few short moments later, Van Endel's phone began ringing.

"Van Endel."

"What do you need, Dick?" Chief Jefferson sounded as out of sorts as Van Endel had guessed he would. "Lanie and I got a room downtown to watch the fireworks out the window, and we're expected in the lounge soon."

"We need to reopen the Molly Peterson investigation. We need to talk to old witnesses. I have a very strong feeling that the girl who was found behind the movie theater isn't Molly. After talking to some sources downtown, I've got a hunch that Molly was one of two girls taken that night, most likely by our man who keeps dumping bodies at Riverside. I want to get your permission to apply for material-witness warrants for every teenager she was with that night, and I want to talk to those three boys they saw her as well."

There was silence from the other end of the phone, and finally, Jefferson spoke.

"Dick, have you been drinking tonight? No offense, but this sounds like you had some sauce and got your noodle a little overdone. Not the end of the world if that's the case, but if—"

"Chief, I'm serious," said Van Endel. "I really want to grill Molly's pals and get them to break. I know they will. As for the boys, I need to hear what they saw. It could be vital to this case. It could mean the difference between that girl living or dying."

"Dick, I think we can have a talk about this on Monday, after the holiday weekend is over, but right now, it's Saturday and my wife's giving me a stink-eye. As for today, I'm going to stick with the assumption you gave me a couple of days ago. If you recall, both you and the coroner agreed that the girl was almost definitely Molly. Also, we do have an inquiry out on that situation, to try and figure out that whole mess with her teeth. As for bothering those kids and stirring up that sort of hornets' nest? Are you out of your mind? We knew those boys were lying, and we still know it.

"Let me guess how this all started. You and the doctor were out talking to that pack of whores-cum-witnesses, and after you either threatened them with arrest or rewarded them with money, they gave you information. Dick, you're a good detective, but your cop-sense needs calibration. Get the ship righted, and we'll talk about this in a couple of days, OK?"

After a long moment of silence, Van Endel sighed. Jefferson was an ass-hat. "All right."

"There you go. I can hear it in your voice, Dick. You need to either start drinking if were dry or stop if you were already wetting your beak. Christ, we've already got the body; leave those people alone. Are we clear?"

"Crystal," said Van Endel, and hung up the phone.

"What did he say?" Dr. Martinez asked, though it was obvious from her eyes that she knew.

"He said that I need to let sleeping dogs lie." He clapped his hand together and stood. "That means no material-witness warrants, and those teenagers are not going to break without them."

"So what are we going to do?"

"We are going to go get a beer. I'm buying. After that, I'm going home, and first thing in the morning I'm going to find those boys and see if they feel like talking to someone who is ready to believe them."

"And apologize," said Dr. Martinez. "You are someone willing to apologize and listen. Where are you buying me a beer? I'd prefer not the Shipwreck."

"Oakway it is."

"Fine," she sighed. "Shipwreck, then. But the fact that you had the name of an even worse bar so handy is not a good thing, Detective."

47

Luke was alone in the fort. The Fourth of July fireworks had finally ground to a stop, and now all that was left to do was to wait for his friends to show up.

Hooper. The name from the mailbox was stuck in his head like a piece of stringy beef between two molars. He was almost sure that he was familiar with the name in some local way, but he couldn't come up with anything, and so the name stayed just a name, rather than a solution. The house seemed a likely enough place for Molly to have been kept, or was possibly even the place she was still being kept, but Luke was no detective, and he knew it. The truth was, their criteria for discovering which house it was had no sort of scientific method. They had decided what they thought the house would be like, but that was based on stupid kid stuff, not on reality.

It was all going to come down to Tim. Luke had decided hours ago that no matter what he came up with, none of it would matter if Tim didn't have info on the car. And even then, if Tim discovered the make or model of the car and it was just a normal car, like a brown sedan or something, even that wouldn't matter.

Not for the first time, Luke wished they had just been believed in the first place. It would have made everything that they'd had to do unnecessary, and they could have just had a normal summer.

He was surprised to find that he missed being at home. He wasn't sure what exactly it was that made him feel that way, because when he thought about all the separate elements of home, none of them made him miss it at all. Still, the thought of his bedroom, and particularly his bed, seemed almost magical compared with the fort. Not that a few days away from it wouldn't make him miss their secret space in the woods, but as for sleeping in it, he'd had enough.

He looked as his watch: they'd be here any minute. As if in answer to the thought, Luke could hear the sounds of feet on the boards of the ladder. He smiled. *Finally.*

Tim came up first, followed immediately by Scott. Both of them wore the smile of the guilty, something Luke had felt on his face a lot lately too. It still sucked not to be trusted, but it was pretty cool to be doing something about it.

He let them get settled, then sat Indian-style in the fort with his friends. "Well?" Luke said. "Don't leave me hanging, I've been bored for like six hours."

"My sister got us some info," said Tim. "Apparently, the guy who took Molly was driving a green Dodge Dart."

"Kind of a boring car for a kidnapper," said Scott. "I expected something cooler. A Dart's like something one of our parents would drive. I guess if that's the car, then that's the car. But it still seems sort of lame." Then Scott perked up and began digging in his left pocket, his hand finally emerging with a nickel-plated revolver. "It's a .38," he said. "Carl says it doesn't kick too bad, or at least that's what he told my mom when he was trying to get her to keep it in her purse."

"Is it loaded?" asked Tim, sounding nervous.

"Of course it is," said Scott. "It holds six bullets. Do either of you want to hold it?"

Tim waved his hand no, but Luke took it from him. It felt cold and a little bit evil to Luke. A rifle could be used for lots of things, but as far as he knew, a pistol like this was used for killing people, and not much else. He handed it back to Scott, handle first.

"I didn't do as well as you guys," said Luke. "Looking for weird houses was way harder than I thought it would be. They pretty much all look a little weird if you don't know the people who live inside of them. There was one that stuck out, though. It had a name on the mailbox. 'Hooper.'"

"Nope, that can't be the one," said Scott, irritated. "That's one of Carl's Vietnam buddies. He's a little weird, but not like that kind of weird."

"What kind of car does he drive?" Luke asked quietly, feeling like he already knew the answer.

When Scott replied, his voice was weak. "I'm pretty sure it's a green Dart, you guys." Luke saw him swallow, or try to. Luke's own mouth had just filled with cotton. "Holy fucking shit," Scott said. "Do you really think it could be him? It just doesn't seem possible that I would know the guy. He's been over like a million times." He put his hand on top of his head and clamped down on it. "You know what, though? He was supposed to come over and help Carl with Mom's car, but he got sick or something."

"Or he kidnapped a girl and got shot for his trouble," said Tim. "We all knew there was a strong possibility that we were going to know the guy who did this. Now it looks like we do, or at least Scott does."

Scott was nodding his head, still holding the top of it, and looking like he might puke.

"So what are we going to do?" Tim asked.

"I'm going to go there tomorrow and knock on the door," said Luke. "When he opens it, I'll know if it's him from how his leg looks."

"Are you nuts?" Tim asked. "What are you going to say? He's probably not going to like getting bugged."

"I'll just tell him I'm running a lawn service, and if he wants his cut by a kid looking to make a little bit of money, I'll do it for $2.50 on a date of his choosing."

"That could work," said Tim. "It's really not a bad idea at all. The mowing thing isn't either. I bet people would for real pay us for that, and we could make some bucks."

"Let's figure this out first," said Luke with a grin. "You two are still under house arrest, no way are your parents going to let you out to go make money. Shit, with all the luck we've had lately, they'd probably make you go do it for free, as, like, a community service or something."

"What if it really is him?" Scott asked quietly. "What if it is Hooper and he just, like, grabs you or something?"

"Easy," said Luke. "I take Carl's gun. If he grabbed me, I really doubt that he'd search me, then I'd just blast him when he turned around. No one would think a kid was coming armed, not even a really crazy person."

"I need to get this back," said Scott, staring down at the gun in his hand, then up at Luke. "You have to promise to bring it back, like, for real promise. If you don't, I'm going to be grounded forever."

"Scott," said Luke. "Of course I'll bring it back. I don't need it for anything except this. Besides, all that's going to happen is he's going to open that door and say no to the lawn mowing. I'll get a look at his leg, and that will be that. We meet up here tomorrow night, I tell you what I saw, and maybe this whole thing is almost done."

"All right," said Scott. He held it out, butt first, to Luke, who took it. It felt somehow heavier in his hand than it had before. "Just be careful with it," Scott said. "Don't shoot yourself or anything."

"I won't," said Luke. "I'm not a complete moron. Though some people might question my choice of friends."

"No jokes," said Tim. "Not now. We meet here tomorrow, same time?"

"Same time," said Luke. "Unless I save Molly tomorrow." He grinned. "Then you guys can see me on the news, and maybe we can hang out again."

48

Tim slipped through the woods, gliding on exhausted legs through the trees. It was odd how the woods had once been so terrifying at night but now were amazing. It was the only place where he felt like himself after everything that had happened. He felt free there, like the world really held possibilities. It was a nice feeling, especially with the patio, the policemen and parents who thought you were a liar looking for attention, and the tyranny and ever-looming danger of the upcoming school year. The woods at night were a peace away from that, in a way that almost didn't make sense. If anything, after he'd seen the man with Molly, the woods should have been terrifying, and the fort less than a fort. If anything, it had had the opposite effect. Tim didn't know what growing up was going to be like, but if it was anything like the freedom of walking alone through a forest, able to do whatever he wanted, it was going to be great. An invisible owl hooted from some impossible perch, and Tim walked home.

He slipped silently across his own lawn and shimmied his body up the window and into the house, much like he would enter the fort off of the ladder. Also like at the fort, Tim found arms pulling him into the house. Unlike the arms of his friends, these were adult, and much more powerful. The light flashed on, and Tim saw that his parents were in his room and his dad was holding him.

"I can explain," said Tim, and in answer, his mom crossed the room and slapped him. The noise of it was more air rifle than .22, and the surprise of it shocked him more than the pain did. His dad released him, and Tim slumped to the floor. Tears ran down Tim's face, and he made no effort to stop them. He was emotionally ruined, and this was the last straw.

"Tammy, we talked about this," said Stan. "We never wanted to hit either one of them, no matter what they did. Every kid makes mistakes. Hopefully Tim will learn from this."

"I hit him for his own good," spat Tammy. "Nothing else works, so why not give it a try? Tim, if ever there was any proof of what a little liar you are, this is it. If you'd actually seen any adult in those woods doing what you said, you never would have gone back there." She paused to catch her breath, and Tim just stared at the floor, the shock of it still settling in. "In case you were wondering, Scott knocked over a table in his room when he came home, and Beth had the good sense to call me. I called Luke's house, but his mom must have slept through the ringer. I don't know what we're going to do, though. You lie, you make up stories—"

"We're going to have a family meeting and discuss this in the morning," said Stan. "We talked about that a few minutes ago, if you recall, Tammy. Tim, get some sleep. We're going to try."

Tim's mom left the room as he got into bed. His dad paused at the door and put his finger on the light switch. "I can explain," said Tim. "I can make it all make sense."

"No you can't," said Stan as he shut off the light. He paused there in the doorway. "To think I almost believed you."

Somehow, that was a thousand times worse than being slapped by his mom.

49

Hooper woke with the sun. He had barely any memories of what had happened the day before, other than being fairly certain that somehow he had survived a VC mortar attack. *I'm shell-shocked, that's what it is.* Clad in only a towel, Hooper dragged his dead leg behind him, not sure if it was better or worse that the pain was still gone.

Once he was in his room, the thought came to him that there was something he needed to do, but he couldn't remember what it was. He came in to dress, though, so he did that. Underwear first, then fatigues. He dropped the revolver in his pocket and then strapped the .45 in its holster to his chest. The pants were so tight on his right leg that the pressure caused his wounded leg to thrum, bringing a dull sensation that was almost pain to it. Hooper used his KA-BAR to split the pants down the shin, from just above his knee to the bottom of the cuff, and the pain and the pressure went away.

Why am I doing this, why am I getting dressed?

Hooper ran a hand over his forehead. The fever that had broken in the night felt like it was coming back, and swiftly. *You're getting dressed to be ready, in case the VC come or you're relieved of duty.* Hooper wasn't sure what to think. He knew he was in his house but also that he was back in the shit, back in the Nam. None of it made any sense. It was terrifying to have no idea what he was supposed to be doing.

You need to relax.

Hooper sat back down on the couch. It was stained with blood, his blood. *I need to get them before they come for me, before they come to take Amy from me.* The thought of Amy was a revelation: once this was all figured out, he needed to go back down there, get her some food and water, and have a conversation. She needed to be told that the VC were in the area, and that even though Charlie was gunning for them, she was going to be safe. If she knew that he was going to help her, she'd probably feel a lot better about everything, might understand why he had to hide her like he was doing. The enemy was everywhere, and she should know that.

Hooper leaned back on the couch, letting the sun come through the drapes and bathe his face in the light. It was wonderful, and the only thing missing was Amy. As soon as this was all settled, things were going to be right. Maybe they could even go outside again together. Not away from the house, of course, but they could go in the backyard with its high fence. Now, though, he needed to be vigilant and hold the house until help came. His guys knew where he was, and it wasn't going to take forever for them to get him out of here, just longer than he wanted them to. That's how it was with Big Green, though, a never-ending waiting game.

His leg was throbbing again, like it had been before he'd sliced his pants, and Hooper decided it was from the pressure of it lying on the couch. He picked his leg up, then spun, so that he was lying on his right side and he could kneel with his hurt leg on the floor. *Fuck, it's cold in here.* He ran a hand across his forehead. Sweat was beading up, and his scalp felt on fire. Letting his hand fall away, he knew that his injuries needed time and rest. He closed his eyes, falling asleep immediately, and was transported back to Vietnam, back to the jungle. They were after him, but he was going to win.

50

Luke woke with the sun. The fort rarely got hot, not truly hot, but it was all but roasting inside this morning. Luke groaned and sat up, then finished the last of the warm Coke he'd brought the day before. It was flat and hot, but better than nothing. Then he took the gun Scott had taken and slid it into his pocket, walked to the ladder, and began to slowly climb down.

It was early, but not too early, and he knew that if he didn't go to that house soon and knock, he'd lose his nerve. If his mom had finally called him in as a runaway, getting picked up with a gun was going to be bad. Letting his friends down because this seemed even scarier now than it had before would be even worse.

He was, after all, the only one of them who could do this. The cops didn't believe them, their parents didn't believe them, his friends were locked away. So Luke felt as if he had no choice but to knock on that door and then decide if he knew what was going on. Still, as he stepped from the ladder to the forest floor, he felt pure terror. His world was changing, and not for the better. The gun had grown yet heavier overnight, and this felt all too real.

He strode through the trees, feeling as though he'd spent the last few days as a ghost, unsure of what he was looking for or why he was even alive at all. The woods were vibrant and alive, and even with the potentially dangerous task before him, Luke felt more in tune with the world than he could recall ever having felt in his life. By the time his feet were on the blacktop headed to Hooper's house, Luke no longer felt scared, nor did he feel like some comic-book version of himself. This was real, and it was something he needed to do.

The house loomed before him in a way that Luke figured was happening to no one else. The closer he got to it, the more mysterious it appeared, turning from just another house in the suburbs into something more than the sum of its parts. *If we're right, that will always be the house where a kidnapped girl was held. The neighbors will tell stories until it's eventually torn down, and whether they rebuild or it remains an empty lot, for as long as this street remains, that will be a marked spot.* It was almost like seeing something that shouldn't have been there, like something impossible. Finally, deciding he was making too much out of it, Luke walked to the front door.

His heart was thrumming in his chest as he knocked on the door with his left fist. His right hand was wrapped tightly around the pistol in his pocket. He waited a few seconds and then heard a loud thump from inside the house, along with someone groaning. The door swung open quickly, and Luke knew at once that he'd picked the right house, and that he'd also made a horrible mistake.

The man standing in the doorway was wearing an army uniform that was ill fitting. Too tight across the belly and chest, but loose in the arms. The pants had been slit up the right leg, and Luke could see puffy, black-and-blue flesh with red tendrils of infection crawling up and out of sight. The man was holding a large black pistol, with an impossibly huge hole at the end of it. His finger was on the trigger, and the gun was shaking. "VC motherfucker," the man said. "Zipper-head cocksucker." He grabbed Luke's arm, and Luke was fumbling with the gun as he was dragged into the house. The man slammed the door behind them, and no one saw any of it.

Luke landed on the floor, and he fought his pants for the revolver. Finally the gun came free and clattered to the floor. The man looked at Luke over his gun, and then to the pistol, back and forth. Luke dove for the weapon, and the man said, "If you touch that heater, I'll put one in your back, Charlie." His voice was gravelly and thick, like he had a mouth full of syrup and marbles. Luke left the gun where it was and sat up, tears streaming down his face. *It wasn't supposed to be like this.*

"Where are the rest of you?" the man asked, and Luke just shook his head. "Where are the rest of the VC? Where are they? I know you were on that sniper team. But guess what? I'm not dead. You missed, VC motherfucker." The man spit on the floor. It was thick and yellow, as though the infection in his leg were eating him up from the inside. Luke ignored it and began trying to inch slowly toward the gun. "Tell me, you fuck. Slope motherfucker. How many are you? What is the plan?"

Luke grabbed for the gun. There was a noise in the room like thunder, the loudest thing he'd ever heard, and then he was back in the fort playing rock-paper-scissors. It was summer and it was wonderful, and then the world went black.

51

Van Endel woke with the sun. He shaved, showered, and ate quickly, and decided as he flipped through his Moleskine that he would stop at Luke Hutchinson's house first. He was the only one of the three boys whom Van Endel hadn't spoken with after he'd initially gotten their permission to talk, and he figured that was as good a place to start as any, especially since the boy's mother had never made an appearance at the station. He was familiar with the area they lived in from his time spent as a uniform breaking up fights and busting drunks. It was one of the low-income spots on the north end.

Van Endel parked the Caprice and checked the address on the trailer with the one in his book. He was at the right place. The house was fairly nondescript and seemed to be in the same state of lazy disrepair as the ones around it—not trashed yet, but on the way there.

He walked down a short path, the heat of the day making beads of sweat appear on his hairline. *Thank God Doc and I really did have only one last night. Weather like this makes even a little hangover unbearable.* Van Endel knocked twice on the door and counted to sixty in his head as nothing happened. He knocked again, harder this time, and for longer. Van Endel gave a look to his watch. It was early, 9:00 a.m., but not crazy early.

There was a noise at the back of the trailer, and then the sound of a door slamming. Curious now, Van Endel walked around back and saw a man with his pants down to his knees attempting to scale a fence surrounding the park.

"Get down right now," said Van Endel, his gun and badge appearing in his hands as easily as taking a breath.

The man did so and began fiddling with his pants, which, as it turned out, were on backward.

"On the ground," said Van Endel. "Forget your pants, buddy, just get your ass down."

The man complied, lying flat on the lawn. Van Endel cuffed him, then stood him up, holstered his pistol, and pulled the man's pants up and buckled them behind his back.

"What in the hell are you doing running?" Van Endel asked as he walked the man around the trailer and back to the Caprice. "Especially running with your pants down?" Van Endel opened the car door and slid the man in, giving a sad look to the state of the man's pants against the clean interior. "C'mon, buddy, out with it. What's going on in there?"

"I didn't have nothing to do with it," the man said. "I was in there fucking Emma, the mother. I didn't touch them kids."

Van Endel shook his head and looked to the trailer. Smoke was coming out of an open window. It wasn't enough to suggest that the house was on fire. It looked more like someone was burning something. Van Endel slammed the car door on the man who claimed to have been fucking Emma, the mother, then took his walkie-talkie from the front seat. The walkie squawked, and Van Endel barked into it where he was and what he was doing. "No clue what I'm walking into, so tell them to hurry."

The smoke was intensifying, so Van Endel left the walkie on the hood of the Caprice, unholstered his pistol, walked to the front door, and kicked it in. Smoke billowed out as he strode in.

Two bored-looking twin girls in their early teens sat watching TV on an old and battered couch. They looked at him and then back to the TV. "Get outside, now," he said, but the twins just ignored him. Van Endel walked past them to the source of the fire.

There was a woman kneeling on the floor of the trailer, busily feeding stacks of photographs into an oven that was billowing smoke. As far as Van Endel could tell when he stepped closer, the pictures were of the little girls in the living room, and they hadn't been taken at Kmart. In the first couple of shots that Van Endel could see, the twins were posing nude with each other, but then he could see others where worse things were happening, with very white-bodied men, both with and without underwear.

"Goddammit," said Van Endel.

The woman kept frantically shoving sheaves of the photos into the oven, so he grabbed her by the shoulder and yanked her onto her ass on the floor, then turned off the oven. Van Endel made himself look calmly around him. There was enough evidence on the floor that he didn't need to empty the still-burning contents and risk setting the floor on fire. The woman was snuffling, but when Van Endel said, "Get up, get your ass outside," she did.

Once they were out of the trailer, Van Endel shoved the woman into the backseat with the man, for lack of a better spot to keep her, then slammed the door closed. The two girls from the couch were standing together just a step or two away on the front stoop, smoking cigarettes. They were younger than Van Endel had initially figured, twelve or thirteen, most likely. "Dispatch, I need CPS and backup now." He looked back at the girls. "Send some EMTs too. And tell them to hurry." He set the walkie-talkie down, shaking his head at just how fucked up the world could be, as the twins smoked and stared through him.

The first squad car was there about three minutes later. He would have been there sooner, the cop driving it explained, but he'd been getting gas about a mile away when the call came through. They loaded the male into the squad car after the uniform had Mirandized the pair, and then Van Endel and the cop, a guy named Mike whom he had seen around before, leaned against the hood of the Caprice.

"Kind of fucked," said Mike, then nodded at the two girls. The smoke had stopped spilling from the house, but not from the twins' mouths.

"Agreed," said Van Endel. "Very much agreed."

"I mean, they're what, like, fourteen, tops?" Mike asked incredulously, and Van Endel just nodded. The whole thing made him sick. "How did you even know to check this place?" Mike asked, and the question made the hackles on the back of Van Endel's neck rise up. *Luke.* Mike was rambling on: "There is a shitload of filth in there. It's a hell of a bust."

"I was here looking for a kid," said Van Endel. Goddammit, he'd forgotten. "Whole separate case, believe it or not. Speaking of which, I need to go ask Mama Bear back there a couple questions. I'll be back."

"Sounds good, but that's crazy that this is just dumb luck," called Mike, as Van Endel walked to the rear door of the Caprice and opened it. The woman wasn't snuffling anymore. She was staring at him with an evil look in her eyes, and he buried the urge to punch her in the face.

"I need to know about your son, Luke," said Van Endel. "Did he stay the night at a friend's house?"

"How the fuck should I know?" said the woman. "He ran off a few days ago. I figured you were coming by to tell me he did something wrong, stole food or some shit."

"He hasn't been home at all?" Van Endel asked with disbelief in his voice. "Why didn't you call the police?"

"Not my problem," said the woman. "He run off, that's the state's problem. He's yours to deal with, and you're welcome to him."

Van Endel considered explaining to her exactly how and why that opinion was incorrect, deciding instead that one of the masochists who worked for CPS might do a better job of explaining it all to her.

"Any idea where he might be?"

"I figure he's probably staying in the tree fort he and his friends built off in those woods," she said, flailing her arm at the visible line of trees.

Van Endel closed the door and walked back to Mike.

"I'm going to follow upon the hunch that brought me out here in the first place and go for a little sightseeing. You mind holding things down for a few minutes?"

"Not at all," said Mike. Van Endel took his walkie-talkie from its place on the hood, shook his head, and headed off to the forest. He was under the canopy in just a few minutes and, not sure of where to walk, started trying to recall some of the tracking skills his dad had taught him on mostly forgettable hunting trips up north. Seeing a path worn by tennis shoes, Van Endel began to follow it, trying to watch up as much as he did down. After about ten minutes walking, Van Endel was at the fort.

"Anybody up there?" Van Endel called, and when there was no response, he walked to one of three ladders built into the trees the platform was supported by. After testing the first rung, Van Endel began to climb, questioning his sanity internally with every rung. Finally at the top, Van Endel was happy to find that there was no injured boy—or, worse—boys waiting for him. There were a few bits of gas-station-food trash, and then he saw something that did catch his eye. *Huh. Bet nobody's folks knew they were shooting a .22 off up here.* He pocketed the brass casing, kicked at the trash, and went back to the ladder to descend it. *Pretty good carpentry work.*

Van Endel made his way back to the trailer quickly. CPS, an ambulance, and two other marked vehicles had been added to the scene since he'd left. He needed to go talk to the other kids now, find Luke, and figure out what they knew.

He found Mike leaning against the car where he'd been before, but the man and woman were gone from the back of the Caprice.

"I had them move them," Mike said when he saw Van Endel looking. "Find your missing kid?"

"Nope," said Van Endel. "You want to do me a solid?"

"Of course, Detective. How can I help?"

"Get this scene buttoned down, call in more help if you need it. I'll help pick up the mess back at the station. That OK with you?"

"Of course," said Mike. "Still looking for your missing boy?"

"It seems that I am."

52

Tim was helping his dad with the patio. Neither had spoken of the night before. Tim's mom and Becca had gone to Kalamazoo for some reason that Tim didn't care about, most likely shopping. As far as he could tell, his additional trouble-making had gotten his sister off the hook almost completely. Somehow, that knowledge was worse than actually being in trouble in the first place, though Tim didn't quite understand how it could be.

Tim was working as a tamper, pounding down the gravel as his dad walked around measuring everything. Lost in this work, his mind focused solely on the compression of pea gravel, Tim didn't see that they had a visitor until his dad said, "Can I help you?" Tim let his arms relax as the tamper slid to the ground and he turned. It was no regular visitor, it was that detective who had decided they were lying, Van Endel.

"You can, assuming I can talk to Tim," said Van Endel, walking up to Tim's dad and shaking hands with him. "I'm not sure if you recall, but we talked briefly at the station downtown. My name is Detective Van Endel. If I remember right, you're Stan Benchley, is that correct?"

"It is," said Stan. "What did he do now—knock off a convenience store? I don't think anything would surprise me at this point. Lay it on me."

The detective looked surprised at Stan's words and tone, and then seemed as if he might be biting back a smile. "Actually," he said, "I'm here to apologize to your boy. I've got a pretty good feeling that your son and his friends have been telling the truth all along, and I need to hear what else he has to say. Would you mind if we went inside?"

Tim's dad had been wrong, as it turned out: the detective had been able to surprise him. In fact, Stan looked as though he'd had the wind knocked out of him.

———

The three of them sat at the dining room table. Van Endel went over their rights, especially Stan's. Stan said it was perfectly fine for them to talk.

"I would have preferred we do this at the station," Van Endel said, "but time is fleeting, and as I've squandered a few days, I'd like to hear exactly what's going on." Van Endel reached in one of his pockets and set a .22 casing on the table. "And please, Tim. Tell me everything."

Staring at the bullet for a few minutes, Tim knew there was no point in lying, not now. Van Endel would know if he did, and this was his chance to come clean, finally, on everything that had transpired over the last few days.

"When we saw that man and Molly, we were playing sniper with a rifle that Scott borrowed from his stepda—"

"Tim!" his dad exclaimed loudly. "What in the hell—"

For the second time that day, Van Endel came to Tim's rescue. "Mr. Benchley, please," he said. "Let me ask your son these questions. You can figure out an appropriate punishment later, but right now Tim needs to help me." Stan sat back in his chair, red in the face, and Van Endel continued. "All right, Tim. Go ahead. You were playing sniper with a rifle. I assume a .22, is that correct?"

"Yes," said Tim. "A .22 that came apart with just a few twists. It was pretty cool. Anyways, we were trying to hit this target, and our air rifles weren't even coming close, so Scott borrowed the rifle. We were each going to get one shot, and that was going to be it. Then we saw the guy with Molly. And…"

"And what, Tim?"

Tim swallowed, or tried to. But there was nothing there to swallow. "We shot him."

Both Van Endel and Tim's dad rocked back against the backs of their chairs. Van Endel's eyebrows had shot up, and Stan's mouth hung open in horror.

"Say again?" Van Endel said softly. "Who shot him?"

"Luke did," said Tim, feeling like the worst traitor in the world for telling the cop exactly what they'd told each other they'd never share with anyone. "He shot him in the right leg."

"Jesus wept," said Stan.

It came out like a river after that, Tim telling Van Endel and Stan every little detail. The midnight meetings, the detective work. It was only when he got to the part about Becca that Tim said, "Dad, I need you to leave the room for a few minutes, OK?"

"No," said Stan flatly. "If there's something that you did that's so awful that you don't want me to hear it, then I feel like I need to more than ever."

Tim understood his dad probably felt like the floor had been yanked out from underneath him, and just wanted to reestablish some parental authority. But it was not to be. "Dad, it's about Becca and Molly," he said. "I'll tell you later, but not now."

There was a long, silent moment between them, and then his dad sighed and stood. Tim could tell he wanted to say something, but that he didn't know quite what. Finally Stan settled on "Just yell if you need me," his voice dull and hollow, before retreating down the hallway.

"They weren't at the drive-in," said Tim.

"I know," said Van Endel. "Downtown, right?"

"Yeah," said Tim, shocked. "But how did you know?"

"I didn't for sure, not until right now. What I don't know is what they were up to."

"They were playing a game, I think," said Tim, and then he told Van Endel exactly what Becca and her friends had been up to, as best he understood it, anyway. He told him about the outfits, the luring of men to the hotel to be robbed, and about Molly getting in a car and disappearing. Tim stared at the table during the telling, his face blazing the entire time, as though somehow it was his fault that everything had happened. When he was finished, though, he felt as though an enormous weight had been lifted off of his shoulders. Then he fell silent, exhausted, and almost unable to believe that he was being trusted by an adult again.

"So what happened after that?" Van Endel asked. "You knew Molly had been taken, you knew how it had been done, and you knew that the man who had done it lived nearby." Van Endel sighed. "You also knew that you couldn't go to the police or to your parents. So you started sneaking out at night."

"Scott and I did. Luke was already out there, living in the fort. He just left his mom a note and took off."

Tim saw a dark shadow pass over the detective's face and then disappear. "So you started gathering clues. What'd you come up with?"

"Well, I already told you. You know, what Becca told me— oh, yeah, and the guy who picked up Molly drove a green car. I should've told you that first!"

"How sure was she about that?"

"Pretty sure, I guess," said Tim. "She seemed pretty sure of it, or at least was sure of what she'd been told." Tim was scared to tell the next part but kept going anyway. "Scott's job was to borrow another gun from his stepdad, a pistol this time. Luke went around looking for houses that seemed suspicious, and it turned out that one that he thought looked creepy was owned by a friend of Scott's stepdad, and the guy, his name is Hooper, drives a green car."

"Where's the house?"

Tim told him, then said, "That's all of it, I guess. I should go over to the tree fort and tell Luke the cops are involved now. He was supposed to go to Hooper's house and, like, fake that he was going door-to-door about lawn mowing, to see if there were any clues."

Van Endel shook his head. "I was just in the fort. Luke wasn't—" Van Endel stood quickly, upsetting his chair and bouncing the table slightly.

"What's wrong?" Tim asked, standing now himself. His dad was running down the hallway, yelling and asking something, but Van Endel was already out the door.

"What happened?" Tim's dad asked as the door banged closed. There was a shriek of tires on pavement, and all Tim could do was stare at his hands. He felt smaller and weaker than he ever had in his life, and if he could have just disappeared at that moment— not died, just never existed at all—he would have chosen to do so, gladly.

53

Van Endel was driving and on the walkie-talkie at the same, pleading with Dispatch for backup at the address Tim had given him, as well as asking for any available information on one Matt Hooper. He was driving the Caprice at speeds on suburban streets that he would have happily seen another officer fined over, if not outright suspended, and he couldn't have cared less. He figured there was a small window he could land in. It was still early in the day. There was always the possibility that Luke had been out getting breakfast, or running around some other part of the woods, or even that Hooper wasn't the man he'd been looking for. Van Endel found that last part impossible to convince himself of, however. He wished there was some way to get his partner, Phil, in the car with him, or if not, a couple of veteran unis with shotguns.

He was there after just a few streets of unsafe driving, and parked the Caprice in front of Hooper's house. Dispatch hadn't gotten back to him on whether or not Hooper had any priors or was a registered firearms owner, but Van Endel didn't care. Tempering his racing heart, or at least attempting to, as he hurried to the door, Van Endel reminded himself that he had no warrant, and nothing more than circumstantial evidence that Matt Hooper was doing anything wrong at all. Keeping that in mind, Van Endel took the Glock from its place in his jacket. Using the butt of the walkie-talkie in his other hand, Van Endel tapped twice on the door, hard, and stepped to the side of the doorway. There was no response. Feeling a moment of déjà vu from the trailer, Van Endel tapped again and peered through the small window in the door. A shoe that looked too small for a man lay on the floor near the door, and Van Endel decided the shoe was worth risking his career over. He backed up, took a deep breath, and charged the door.

The door opened on the third charge, and Van Endel all but fell into the house. The shoe he'd seen had a match: it was on the right foot of a boy Van Endel was fairly certain was Luke Hutchinson. In addition to the shoe, the boy was also wearing a gunshot wound in his chest, and blood covered the floor. His chest was rising and falling in shallow breaths, and for a very brief moment, Van Endel was unsure of what to do. Then he flattened himself to the wall and checked the first corner. He could see through the kitchen. The sliding glass door at the rear of the house was open, as was the gate at the back of the property. Hooper was in the woods.

Van Endel dropped down next to Luke and placed his gun on the floor, then felt the boy's throat for a pulse. It was there, but weak, and Luke's eyes fluttered at his touch.

"Dispatch, I need backup and EMTs now!" Van Endel screamed into the walkie. The police code that he had known and used for years was gone. It was hard to even form the words. "I've got at least one gunshot wound in a minor. The shooter's looking like he's headed off into the woods behind the house."

"Sending over additional units right now."

"They need to hurry! This kid is bleeding out right now!"

Van Endel set the walkie-talkie down. He could hear sirens over the radio, coming from the trailer park, Van Endel assumed. Guilt powered through him along with the adrenaline. A lot of this was going to come down on him, and that was OK. They'd all made mistakes, but the pale boy on the floor wasn't going to get to complain about them if the EMTs didn't hurry up and get there.

Less than two minutes later, an impossibly long time to sit beside a seemingly doomed boy, the first officers arrived, and as Van Endel had expected, they were from the trailer park scene. For all Van Endel knew, they could even still have a suspect in the back of their squad car, not that he cared either way. The cops came in with guns out, and one of them knelt by Luke. Van Endel knew the cop had been a medic in the service, so at least that much help for the boy had arrived.

Van Endel stood, grabbing his Glock from where he'd left it on the floor. "The suspect is in the woods," he said. "I'm sure of it. The house isn't clear, so proceed with caution." The shell-shocked officer whose partner was attending to Luke just nodded, and then Van Endel was out the back door and running, charging toward the woods with his pistol in his hand, the shame of being so wrong slowly being replaced with rage.

54

Hooper had no choice but to abandon the position at the house. He'd struggled with the choice, but if they were brash enough to just walk up on him like that, who knew what they might try? He'd wanted to bring Amy with him, but it hadn't been possible. She wouldn't move when he'd gone down to the basement, and there was no way he could carry her, not with his injuries. The leg was bad enough, but the fever was making everything so difficult, even focusing on a simple task had become nearly impossible. That changed when he got to the woods.

He knew if he could make the abandoned VC sniper's position he'd be fine. It was easily defensible, even with a handgun, and if more of them came there, he'd be ready. It was hard to move quickly in the woods with his leg, but he had to do it if he was to survive. He was dripping with sweat and almost there when he heard running behind him, crushing fallen sticks and leaves as they ran through the forest. There was no way it could have been a coincidence—they were already coming for him. Hooper increased his pace but allowed himself to look back over his shoulder every few steps. The noise was only getting louder, and then a dark form emerged from the popples he'd hidden in with Amy. Hooper drew the 1911 and fired twice at the form.

The man in pursuit of him was holding a pistol and dressed in a suit. *VC officer, most likely.* Hooper didn't know if he'd hit the man or not, but the pussy was hiding behind a tree and Hooper couldn't get another shot at him. Turning his head, Hooper could see the fort. He fired twice into the tree where the dink motherfucker was hiding, and then began moving as quickly as he could toward the fort. He stopped to catch his breath, and he was close to it, almost in its shadow.

"Matt Hooper!" called the officer. "Surrender now or I will be forced to use deadly force! You need to drop the gun now!" Hooper could hear more noise now, more men entering the woods. "Drop your gun!" called the officer again, and Hooper shot at him three more times in return, locking the bolt back on the semiauto. Hooper hit the magazine eject and let the mag fall to the forest floor. He replaced it, looking up as the VC officer moved closer to hide behind another tree. Hooper fired twice more, then left the tree behind. He could see more VC appearing like ghosts from the popples.

Hooper fired twice over his shoulder as he ran, and he could feel and hear bullets tugging the air around him. Then he was at the ladder. Something in his leg had burst, and he could feel it draining a too-hot liquid down his calf and over his shoe. Ignoring it, Hooper holstered the 1911 and began to climb, his arms forced to do all of the work as his dead leg swung back and forth. He could see the opening at the top when a voice from below called to him.

"Hooper, come down now! I've got you dead to rights, just get down so this can end!" Hooper ignored the VC officer, though he did look back at him. The man was pointing a black pistol at him. Hooper drew the 1911 and then felt something hit him hard, twice, in the chest. He dropped the gun as a third punch was delivered to his body. All sound was gone, and Hooper let go of the tree. He fell to the ground, and the war was over.

55

Van Endel hovered over the body. He was waiting for the rest of the cops to catch up to him before he attempted to secure Hooper. Seeing the leg injury up close, Van Endel was shocked the man had been able to move as quickly as he had. Red lines of infection ran up the leg as far as Van Endel could see, and he had no desire to inspect it further.

Van Endel thought of the boy he'd left in his house, and didn't want to imagine what else a thorough inspection might find.

Finally, two uniformed cops caught up to him, his friend Walt Summers, who was breathing far too hard for a man his age, and Mike, from the trailer park. "I'll keep a gun on him," he told them. "Cuff and flip him so we can see if he's still kicking."

Walt leaned against the tree Hooper had fallen from while Mike cuffed Hooper, then turned him. Van Endel didn't check for a pulse, nor did he need to. There were three ragged holes punched in Hooper's chest, two of them right over his heart, the other one a few inches below. Any of the three would have been a likely kill shot; the three combined were a guarantee. Van Endel smiled thinly.

"Leave everything as it is," he said in a very tired voice. "Don't touch shell casings or anything else. Just keep everyone away until some of the lab guys get down here. You OK, Walt?"

"I'm fine, Dick. That was just a long, nerve-racking run. Been a long time since I got shot at, and I have to say it was exactly as much fun as I remembered it to be."

"That was good shooting, Detective," said Mike. "But we've got this under control. You go head on back up and call it in."

"Thanks," said Van Endel, and he began walking away from the fort. When he looked back at them, it almost looked like Walt and Mike were paying Hooper their last respects, but of course they weren't.

By the time he got back to the fenced-in yard, he was exhausted and covered in burrs. He brushed himself off as well as he was able but felt as though he was just moving the burrs around. He made the house and could see before he even walked in that it was swarming with cops. *Gonna be like this for a while.*

Van Endel walked to the front room where Luke had been, and an anonymous voice said, "You get him?"

"He's dead."

There was no celebration, but Van Endel felt hands patting his back and muted voices saying things like "Good job" and "Nice work." Van Endel ignored them and finally made the front room. Luke was gone, but his blood wasn't.

Van Endel grabbed his walkie-talkie from the floor and headed outside to call Dispatch and have them ring Jefferson. The chief was going to have to take a break from the holiday weekend, whether he liked it or not. Van Endel's hands were starting to shake as he stepped through the front door.

Two gurneys were being loaded into separate ambulances.

"Somebody else get hurt?" he asked no one in particular, and one of the cops milling about said, "They got the kid from the front room and the Peterson girl."

Van Endel felt like he was in a dream. "Molly was in there? Is she still alive?"

"She is right now," said the cop, and another finished for him. "But she ain't doing good. Looks like he locked her up in the basement for a week and just forgot about her."

Van Endel sat on the paved stoop at the front of the house and ran his fingers through his hair. *This is all my fault.*

56

The boy's funeral took place four days later. Van Endel was there, and rather than receiving the crucifixion he felt he deserved for being wrong, he'd been lauded both publicly and professionally—he was a hero cop like in the movies, when he'd never felt less like a hero in his life. He sat alone during the service and then stood alone during the burial. People gave him looks. From men, polite nods that said, "Good job"; from women, smiles that seemed to mean more than just that.

Although the investigation was still ongoing, Matt Hooper was believed to be the Riverside killer, as well as the abductor of Molly Peterson, murderer of the still-unknown girl found by the drive-in fence, and killer of Luke Hutchinson, who had died on the way to the hospital, despite the best efforts of the EMTs.

Van Endel certainly felt no regret for the death of Hooper. If anything, he'd saved everyone a lot of bullshit by killing the asshole who had cataloged, in his own meticulous journal, the deaths of fourteen women in Riverside Park. Seeing Luke's weeping mother in jail had been bad, and watching her here with a guard was rotten as well. *Maybe she does care a little bit. Maybe.* As much as he blamed himself for the death of Luke, loser in what had to have been a game of minutes, he blamed her as well, and not just for her son's death.

Molly Peterson had survived her abduction and imprisonment and, against what Van Endel imagined had to have been the advice of her doctors, was in attendance. If Van Endel had needed any convincing on that point, watching her tearfully run a hand over the boy's coffin from her wheelchair and then drop a handful of rose petals over it would've made clear who the real hero was. Luke had died trying, but he had saved the girl. Van Endel had caught the bad guy, but what did that matter now?

Finally the coffin was in the hole and dirt was pitched over it, and Van Endel walked away from it. He'd come with Dr. Martinez, but she was off doing her own thing, and she could meet him at the car. He'd had enough of death for one summer. The fact that there weren't two funerals should have felt like a blessing, and maybe it would later, but it didn't right now. He'd committed the worst kind of failure, and Van Endel had no idea how he was ever going to put his badge back on and do his job. Not because of the shooting, but because of the dead boy who'd been forced to do his job for him.

Van Endel was almost to his car, and the flask that was in it, when a voice called to him from behind.

"Detective?"

Van Endel spun. It was Luke's two friends Tim and Scott. He walked to them. They were alone, their parents likely talking about the tragedy and trying to forget that their sons could just as easily have been killed too.

"How long are you going to be a detective?" Tim asked.

Van Endel wasn't sure quite what to say to this but found himself answering. "I'd always figured my whole life," he said, "but now I'm not so sure. Today it seems that my calling might be elsewhere, or ought to be."

"You're a good cop," said Tim, while Scott nodded. "At least as far as we can tell."

His voice thick, Van Endel said, "Thanks for that."

"But do you see our eyes?" Tim asked.

Van Endel nodded, looking back and forth between them and seeing no hatred or anger, just the eyes of two sad children who would be forced into being men soon enough.

"I do," said Van Endel.

"Well," said Tim, "you should keep being a detective, but you should remember us. Remember that even when it seems impossible, people can still be telling the truth."

"I will," said Van Endel, but the boys were already leaving, their backs to him.

57

It was nearly twenty years later when Van Endel thought of them yet again. It wasn't the first time that he'd recalled the boys while working a case. Tim and Scott, all grown now, of course, had influenced his career more than he thought they ever would have imagined.

Now, though, it was like they were in the room with him, along with Luke. Phil, his old partner, had died of a heart attack three years prior, and so his new partner, Tom, sat with him. But more than Tom, and more than the suspect before them, it was the boys whom Van Endel felt in the room with him. They were electric around him, and it was all he could do not to ask Tom or the suspect if they could feel or see something weird.

He didn't, though. Instead he let the suspect, some tattooed scumbag named Mike, tell the story of how his drug-addicted girlfriend named Sid had killed herself in the tattoo shop above where he worked. Tom had said from the start that he was positive that Mike had done it, and so had Van Endel. Now, he wasn't so sure. In fact, he thought they might be mistaking the man's guilt over not being there for his girl as his guilt over her death.

"Tell it all to me again," said Van Endel as he looked deep into the suspect's eyes and saw the same thing, that same electricity he'd seen so many years before. The man began talking, but Van Endel already knew he was telling the truth. He knew exactly what to look for.

ACKNOWLEDGMENTS

My first four novels were dedicated to lives taken far too young, and it is with no small amount of pleasure that I'm able to say that thankfully there appears to be a drought in my life of young people falling far before their time. I truly hope that is a streak that lasts a good long while. For my daughter, Scout, someday when you read this, I hope it gives you fond memories of the time in your life when this was written. You were eight when this manuscript was begun, nine when I was editing it, and nearly ten when it went to press. I hope you are as happy when you read this as you were on the days when I wrote it. I love you very much and cannot wait to talk to you after you read this. Considering the content, I'd say we have a few years yet to go.

Thanks to my wonderful wife, Megan, who has endured a whirlwind of writing that no one should have to live through, yet you've done it with a smile on your face. We've had a long journey together, and I'm blessed to have traveled this road with you at my side.

Thank you to my parents, both of whom were first readers this time around, and who offered wonderful advice that helped this story be everything that it could at that stage of its creation.

I respect you both so much for the lives you've lived, and I could never thank you enough for putting books in my hands at a young age. Reading, and now writing, has been my lifeblood, and always will be.

A massive thank-you goes to Amazon editor Terry, who gave me a chance when no one else was interested in my writing. I am blessed to have such a thoughtful man overseeing my writing career, and there is not a day that goes by when I don't think about the ways that you have changed the lives of my family, and about how lucky I am to count you as a friend.

Thank you to my partner in crime, creative editor David, who has helped all of my books get ready for the eyes of the public. We form a powerful collaborative team, and the edits for *The Fort* came in such a short and spastic amount of time that I don't really feel comfortable saying just how quickly the book was made ready. Better than the speed, though, is the quality that your work brings to my writing. You see things that I don't, and my writing improves dramatically with just a few of your keystrokes helping to guide the way.

Thanks to my friend Jacque, as always. The tremendous amount of work you do for your authors could never be overstated, and in case you ever forget, we appreciate the hell out of it. As a very influential man once said, "Family. Religion. Friendship. These are the three demons you must slay if you wish to succeed in business." As an aside, we should be going to B-Con a few months after this comes out, and that will be super rad.

To my dear friend Sarah Burningham of Little Bird Publicity, the early word on the street was that we would be working on this one together. If we did, I'm sure we had a lovely time; if not, I'm sure we'll get the band back together soon enough. All that aside, I hope you and your baby—over six months old when this comes out!—are doing wonderfully, and sleeping wonderfully as well.

To Greg, who helped immeasurably with a spot of writer's indecisiveness that was plaguing the end of the second act of this story, and helped breathe fire into the third, all of my first readers are appreciated, but you knocked this one out of the park, and for that I thank you.

To everyone else at Amazon, thank you all so much for your continued efforts on my behalf, and on the behalf of your other authors. I never would have guessed that I would find so many friends in the world of writing, but with you that is exactly what I have. In no particular order, Sarah, Andrew, Katie, Alan, Grace, Rory, Justin, Megan, Patrick, David, Jessica, Ashley, Luke, and everyone else at Amazon and Brilliance Audio, thank you all so very much.

Finally, thanks to you, my readers, for the chance to tell a story. I hope we get to hang out again sometime.

ABOUT THE AUTHOR

Photograph by Megan Davis, 2012

Born in Ithaca, New York, Aric Davis has lived most of his life in Grand Rapids, Michigan. He is the author of *A Good and Useful Hurt* and the acclaimed YA novel *Nickel Plated*, called by Gillian Flynn a "dark but humane, chilling and sometimes heart-breaking work of noir" and given a "Top 10" *Booklist* designation in 2011. A punk-music and tattoo aficionado, Davis has been a professional body piercer for sixteen years. He and his wife and daughter live in the chilly Midwest, where they can enjoy roller coasters, hockey, and cold weather.